Puffin B

A peek at the UNSEEN . . .
This is unbelievable.
This is unreal.

What is going on here?
First I get a toilet seat stuck around
my face and now this little parrot is
following me around.

Unseen events like . . .
the dead coming back to life
escaping a man-eating ghost
growing spare fingers
cheating the fate that awaits you

FROM THE ONE AND ONLY PAUL JENNINGS

also by paul jennings

More information about Paul and his books can be found at
www.pauljennings.com.au *and* puffin.com.au

PAUL JENNINGS

¡Unseen!

not scary

PUFFIN BOOKS

PUFFIN BOOKS

Published by the Penguin Group
Penguin Group (Australia)
250 Camberwell Road, Camberwell, Victoria 3124, Australia
(a division of Pearson Australia Group Pty Ltd)
Penguin Group (USA) Inc.
375 Hudson Street, New York, New York 10014, USA
Penguin Group (Canada)
90 Eglinton Avenue East, Suite 700, Toronto ON M4P 2Y3, Canada
(a division of Pearson Penguin Canada Inc.)
Penguin Books Ltd
80 Strand, London WC2R 0RL, England
Penguin Ireland
25 St Stephen's Green, Dublin 2, Ireland
(a division of Penguin Books Ltd)
Penguin Books India Pvt Ltd
11, Community Centre, Panchsheel Park, New Delhi-110 017, India
Penguin Group (NZ)
67 Apollo Drive, Rosedale, North Shore 0632, New Zealand
(a division of Pearson New Zealand Ltd)
Penguin Books (South Africa) (Pty) Ltd
24 Sturdee Avenue, Rosebank, Johannesburg 2196, South Africa

Penguin Books Ltd, Registered Offices: 80 Strand, London WC2R 0RL, England

First published by Penguin Books Australia, 1998
This edition published 2003

Text designed by George Dale, Penguin Design Studio
Typeset in Berkeley Old Style by Midland Typesetters, Maryborough, Victoria
Printed in China

National Library of Australia
Cataloguing-in-Publication data:

Jennings, Paul, 1943–
    Unseen.
    ISBN 978 0 14 130515 8.
    I. Title.
A823.3

puffin.com.au
www.pauljennings.com.au

The words from `The Black Velvet Band', which appear on
pages 144 and 154, are reproduced from A Treasury of
Favourite Australian Songs, compiled by Thérèse Radic and
published by Penguin Books Australia in 1983.

For Claire

Contents

Contents

One-Finger Salute

Every day after school Gumble sticks his finger up at me. Every day. He sits on the fence at the end of our street and gives me the one-finger salute. He has a bunch of toughs for friends and they all laugh like crazy every time he does it.

It might not sound like much. A one-finger salute. I mean it doesn't actually cause pain. Not like getting your ear twisted or your arm shoved up behind your back. But it hurts all the same. It hurts my feelings.

I can't stop thinking about it. It's like a stone in my shoe. Or a dog barking in the night. All day at school I'm thinking about the one-finger salute Gumble will give me on the way home tonight.

My dad says it's extremely rude to stick your middle finger up in the air at someone.

And I personally have never done it.

Don't get me wrong. I'm no angel. But there are

a number of reasons why I don't stick my middle finger up at Gumble.

1. He's bigger than me.
2. He has really mean mates who would make my life even more miserable than usual.
3. I don't have any middle fingers to stick up at him.

The last reason is the main one I don't do it.

So here I am. Walking home from school. And there are Gumble and Smithy and Packman sitting on the fence, waiting.

'Hey, Digit,' yells Gumble. 'Cop this.' He sticks his middle finger up in the air and starts moving it up and down in a very insulting way. Smithy and Packman start doing it too. They laugh like crazy.

I walk by, hating them as usual. What can I do? I could stick my little finger up at them. I could stick my thumb up at them. I could even stick my ring finger up at them. But it's just not the same. You have to stick the middle finger up. The big finger is the one that gives the big insult.

I hurry off down the street. I'm mad and embarrassed. Their insults follow me down the street like a cloud of flies. Even after I reach home I can hear their laughter ringing in my head.

2

I look at my hands. Eight fingers. Or six fingers and two thumbs if you want to look at it that way.

I started off with ten fingers but lost two of them when I was a little kid.

I was only three at the time. Mr Watson, the guy next-door, was cutting his lawn. He left the motor of his lawn-mower running and went round to the backyard to empty the grass clippings. I wandered over to the lawn-mower and stuck my hands underneath to see what was whizzing around under there.

That's what I was told I did anyway. I actually don't remember anything about it. But my mum and dad do. They rushed me to hospital. Nothing could be done. My two middle fingers were cut right off. They were so mangled that they couldn't be sewn back on.

Mr Watson moved away to another house. It wasn't his fault, but he felt bad every time he saw me. He couldn't bear to think about it.

I don't really blame him. You shouldn't go putting your hands under lawn-mowers.

3

So here I am back in school. Another day with the long walk home at the end of it. Another day to get the one-finger salute from Gumble.

I *should* feel happy. I got eighteen out of thirty for maths today. That's good for me. And Mrs Henderson put my science project up on the wall. So I *should* be smiling. But I'm not.

Instead I spend every second thinking about paying back Gumble for picking on me. I'll get even with him if it kills me.

I can't stick my middle finger up at him so I'll have to think of something else.

It's free-reading time and I start to leaf through my scrapbook. I've read it a thousand times.

But I read it again.

I start with the bit about worms. It's really interesting. You know what happens when a worm sticks its head out of the ground and a bird grabs it? The worm hangs on. It doesn't want to be breakfast for a bird. So the bird pulls and the worm squirms. The bird pulls more and the worm starts to stretch like an elastic band. Something has to give. And it does.

Twang, the worm breaks in half. The bird eats its end and flies off.

And then. Wait for it. This is the good bit. The worm grows a new tail.

I turn the pages. Now this is really weird. There is a type of frog that can grow new toes. I look down at the pictures and shake my head. I wish I was a frog like that.

See, I have all these clippings in my scrapbook.

And I have something else as well. In my bedroom at home. In an empty ice-cream container. Yes, I have a drop-tail lizard. A live one.

If a kookaburra grabs a drop-tail the lizard drops its tail. The kookaburras just can't catch the whole drop-tail lizard. All they get is its tail.

Drop your tail and run away – live to fight another day. That's the drop-tail lizard.

But, even better than that. The fantastic thing is –

The lizard grows another tail.

Now, why can't people be like that?

Just imagine it. I mean it would change history. Henry the Eighth chops off his wife's head. And she grows a new one. Ace.

4

It's time to walk home, but today Elaine walks with me. She's the girl next-door. She moved in when Mr Watson moved out.

Elaine's not bad for a girl. When she smiles her freckles all bunch up and I feel like reaching out and touching them. With my eight fingers.

Thinking about Elaine makes time fly for once. Before I know it we've come to our street. There's no sign of Gumble. I start to feel good, like I'm walking on air. For once I'll get home without any hassle.

But wait. What's that sticking up over the fence? It's an arm. And a hand. And a finger.

He's doing it again. He's giving me the one-finger salute.

There's another arm. And another. There's laughing. And sniggering. My face goes red. How I'd love to do it back. How I'd love to grab Gumble's arm and shove it behind his back until he squeals. But there are too many of them. I don't have the guts.

Elaine does though. She jumps up and grabs one of the fingers. Then she twists it. She twists it real hard.

There is an enormous scream. 'Ow. Ouch. Let go. Let go.'

She's got Gumble. I'd know that voice anywhere.

She twists his finger until she can't twist it any longer. Gumble's head pops up over the fence. I start to run.

'You're history, Digit,' yells Gumble. 'You're dead meat.'

Elaine runs after me, laughing. It's all right for her. They think I did it. I'm the one who'll be dead meat.

'That showed 'em,' she says. She laughs and all her freckles bunch up. My stomach turns over.

I wish I could impress Elaine. I wish I could pay Gumble back. But I just don't have the fingers for it.

'See you tomorrow,' I say. I walk inside with love and hate buzzing around inside me. And the love isn't for Gumble, I can tell you that.

5

No one's home. Mum and Dad aren't back from work yet. My cat, Slurp, is there, looking for something to eat as usual. I love Slurp partly because she has a similar problem to me. Missing parts. She has no ears. They were ripped off by the dog next-door in a fight. A big mongrel with no tail.

I go to my bedroom and lock Slurp out. Then I take my lizard out of the ice-cream container. His name is Droplet. I make sure that I don't pick him up by the tail. I don't want him dropping it on me.

No, really I don't.

I put him on the floor and watch him run around. He really is the cutest lizard. Outside, Slurp starts to meow. She would love to get in and eat Droplet. She'll eat anything. I open the door and peer out.

'No way,' I yell. 'Go and find yourself a mouse.'

Flash. Whizz. Pow. Oh, no. Slurp shoots across the room after Droplet. Quick as a flash she pins him down by the tail.

And quick as a flash Droplet drops his tail and runs under the bed. The tail squirms and squiggles under Slurp's paw.

I grab Slurp and lock the silly cat in the laundry. 'Bad girl,' I say.

Then I crawl under the bed. Poor Droplet is hiding under a pair of underpants. I gently grab him and hold him in the palm of my hand. Now he has a stumpy little tail instead of a long pointed one.

It doesn't hurt them when they drop their tails, though. Drop-tail lizards are meant to do that. It's just nature.

All the same, I decide to give the little lizard his freedom. I walk out into the garden and put Droplet in the flower-bed. 'Bye, Droplet,' I say. 'Don't worry about it. You're going to grow a new tail.' He wriggles off into the bushes. 'Drop in any time,' I say.

I go back to my bedroom and shut the door. I look at the lizard's tail lying there on the floor. It's still wriggling and jiggling like a crazy worm. After a bit it stops. I get an idea.

No. Look, I'll be honest. The idea came to me a long time ago but I couldn't pick Droplet up by the tail on purpose. Not pull off his tail. I just couldn't. But now it's happened anyway. By accident. So I might as well give my idea a try.

I carefully pick up the lizard's tail and take it into the kitchen.

I put it on a plate and stare at it. Can I do it, though?

I get out some pepper and salt. And a bit of bread. I shake the tomato sauce all over the tail. This isn't going to be easy. Or pleasant.

But I have to do it. It's the only way.

I take out a very sharp knife.

No. No, no, no. I can't do that. I can't cut it up. Not when it's still wriggling around. It's too awful.

Suddenly I grab the tail. I close my eyes. I shove the tail into my mouth and swallow. Straight down without chewing. The tail has gone to a better place.

Oh, wow. My stomach turns over. And it's not because of Elaine because Elaine isn't even here. The tail gives a couple of squiggles inside me. Then it lies still.

What have I done? Why have I done it? Will it work?

I don't know the answer to all these questions. But I do know one thing. I will never ever tell anyone that I ate Droplet's tail.

6

I go to bed early and I toss and turn and have a terrible dream about an octopus.

When I wake up my whole world has changed. At first I think it's still the dream. Then I wonder if I've gone crazy.

I look at my hands. I just can't believe what I see. I have ten fingers. Yes. Ten fingers. I've grown a new one on each hand. Both of them are perfect.

Gently I touch them. They feel normal. They look normal. I bend one, very carefully. Yes, it works. I touch my nose. I scratch my ear.

'Yes, yes, yes.' It worked. The lizard's tail has done the trick.

I want to rush out to tell Mum and Dad. I want all my friends to know. I want to scream it to the world. 'I've got new fingers.'

But then I stop and think.

No. There's one person I want to see my fingers first. And he's not a friend. No way.

I get dressed, bolt my breakfast and race out of the door. If I'm quick I'll be able to catch Gumble.

There he is, sauntering along with his mates. Elaine's on the other side of the street.

Gumble hears me coming up behind him. He turns and grins.

Then he does it. Yes, just like I knew he would.

'Cop this,' says Gumble.

He gives me the one-finger salute.

And . . .

And . . .

Oh, yes.

I give it back.

I stick the new finger on my right hand up and give the first one-finger salute of my life. Brilliant. Elaine's eyes nearly pop out of her head.

Gumble doesn't think it's brilliant.

He scowls. He growls. He can't believe what he's seeing. He thinks it's a trick. He thinks I've made fake fingers out of clay or plastic or something.

I hold up both of my new middle fingers and wiggle them around. I put them right up under his nose.

Oh, this is good. All my life I've wanted to get even and do this back to Gumble.

Quick as a flash Gumble moves. He grabs my new fingers to see if they're fakes.

I grin. 'They're real,' I say. 'Real, real, real.'

Gumble yanks my fingers.

Splot.

My new fingers break away.

Gumble looks at his hands and grins. He thinks that he's pulled off fake fingers. But he hasn't. They're real. Flesh and blood. Two knuckles on each. And little bones sticking out of the end. Gumble stares at them carefully. Then he starts to scream. The fingers are squirming and worming around in his hands. Just like the lizard's tail.

Gumble's mates start to scream too. They shriek like they've just seen a headless ghost. Gumble throws the fingers into the air and watches in horror as they land on the ground and twist around with a life of their own.

Gumble and Smithy and Packman turn and run. They just run screaming down the road to school. I pick up my new fingers. They won't go back on no matter what I do.

I look at my hands. The stumps have already healed over. I'm back where I was before. Eight fingers. Useless.

By the time I get to school I feel a bit better. After all, I don't think Gumble will give me the one-finger salute again.

And I'm right. He's terrified of me. He knows that he's ripped my fingers off. He thinks he's going crazy. He's too scared to come near me.

There's nothing to worry about any more. Especially when I see what's happening to me. Yes, it's happening. Right in front of my eyes. I'm growing another pair of middle fingers. Awesome. I'm stoked.

7

All day long at school I keep my new fingers to myself. I'm not going to rush into things. Life could be complicated with drop-tail fingers. So I don't want anyone to know about them. Not just yet.

I think about what's happened. This morning I ate a drop-tail lizard's tail. And now I've grown removable middle fingers. One pull and off they come.

Okay, so new ones grow straight away. Just like the tails on lizards.

In one way it's great. But in another way it's not. I'm the only person in the world who can grow new fingers.

Maybe I'm a freak.

I could be on television. In the papers. Everyone will want to see the teenager who can grow new fingers. People will gawk at me. They might even laugh.

I don't want everyone looking at me like I'm the Elephant Man in a sideshow. So I keep my secret to myself. And my hands in my pockets.

Gumble and his mates can't figure it out. Now they're not so sure that they did pull my fingers off this morning. And I'm not telling them anything.

At lunch time I go into the loo and sit down in one of the cubicles. I take my two spare fingers out of my pocket and look at them.

Gumble pulled them off and ran away screaming. No wonder. The fingers still give a little wriggle every now and then. They've been doing this all morning. I've seen people looking at me and wondering what's going on in my pants. It's very difficult to explain.

What am I going to do with these fingers? They're part of me. I can't just flush them down the loo.

I'd like to give them a proper burial. I'd like to say a few words before they're interred. But I can't bury them while they're still wriggling. I'll have to wait until they are well and truly dead.

8

After school I walk home alone with my secret.

Mum asked me to stop off at Knox City Shopping Centre and buy food for Slurp. I make my way to the pet shop and get some chicken loaf. Then I take the escalator up to the first floor.

Is it my imagination or are people staring at me? The people on the down escalator seem to be grinning as they go by. I turn around and see them peering back.

What are they looking at? What's wrong with me? Do I have a big pimple on my nose or something?

I touch my face. With my four fingers.

One of my fingers has gone. It's fallen off. But where is it? I look down the escalator. It's nowhere to be seen.

It must be back down below, wriggling around on the floor somewhere. I have to find it quickly. If someone picks up a human finger they'll take it to the police and everyone will know I'm a freak.

I turn around and start running down the up-escalator. As I go people jump out of the way.

'Disgusting,' says an old man.

'Aaagh,' screams a little girl.

I reach the bottom of the escalator and look around to find that everybody in the whole world is staring at me. Some are laughing but most are just gawping.

Both hands are in my pockets. I move my fingers around and discover something else. The other finger's gone too. They've both gone and new ones are growing. But that's not what everyone's looking at. They can't see my hands inside my pockets.

16

So what *are* they staring at?

I race over to a shop window and peer at my reflection.

Oh, no, no, no. Horrible, horrible, horrible.

One finger has come off in my earhole. It's sticking out from my head and twitching around like a bit of live sausage.

Everyone's laughing and screaming. One kid's putting his finger into his mouth, making out he's going to puke.

This can't be for real. I feel like puking too.

I pull the finger out of my ear and turn and run.

My nose starts to itch. Right up inside. I'm not thinking clearly. If I was I wouldn't do the next stupid thing.

Pick my nose.

Now the crowds are shrieking with laughter and yelling about how revolting I am.

I look in a shop window and see the other finger hanging out of my nose.

I pull it out and bolt out of the entrance.

9

It's a long way home from Knox City and I'm out of breath. My feet hurt and my T-shirt feels like armour around my chest. My underpants are riding up and cutting into me. But I keep running. I just want to get home.

I bunch up my fists and swing my arms as I run. I can see that my two new fingers have already grown.

And in my pockets are four spare fingers. They're twitching and twisting like worms on a hook.

This thing's going mad. I have to tell Mum what's happened. She won't tell anyone or let it get into the newspapers.

I hope.

Finally I reach our street. Home.

But not quite. Sitting on our front fence is Elaine. She gives me a big smile. Which turns into a grin. Which turns into a laugh. My stomach feels queasy, but it's not because of her freckles.

'What's so funny?' I say.

'There's something sticking out of your bottom,' Elaine says politely.

'What?' I say. I feel the blood draining out of me

as I realise what's happened. Oh, please don't let it be true.

While I was running I must have scratched . . .

I feel behind me. I did. It's true. The worst thing in the world. Oh, horror. A finger is sticking out of the crack in my backside. It must have come off when I scratched at my tight jeans. I've run all the way home with a finger sticking out of my bum.

I pull my finger out and run inside without a word.

All I can think about are these stupid fingers. I don't want fingers that come off. I just want to go back to like I was before with one finger missing from each hand.

Eight fingers isn't so bad.

Outside, Slurp is clawing at the door and meowing. She wants to come in. I throw up the window and yell. 'Shut up. Buzz off.'

I've never ever spoken to Slurp like that before. I love Slurp. Now I feel guilty because she's slinking off with her tail between her legs.

I sit on the bed and stare at my hands. One has five fingers and the other four.

I wiggle the horrible drop-tail finger. I don't want it. I hate it.

I grab the finger. And pull. *Splot*. It comes off and starts to wiggle around. I throw it angrily onto the bed and pull the other spare fingers out of my pocket.

I put those five spare fingers on my bed too. Sometimes one or two of them give a bit of a twitch.

I hold my hands in front of my face. Now they're both the same. Four fingers on each hand. But for how long?

I wait for the new fingers to grow.

Minutes pass. Hours pass. Nothing happens.

Brilliant. Wow. Oh, yes. No new fingers are growing. I must have used them all up. Even a drop-tail lizard must run out of tails some time.

Clunk. I hear the front door. Mum's home.

I run downstairs, yelling as I go, 'Mum, Mum, guess what happened.'

10

Mum listens very carefully to the whole tale. 'Very clever, dear,' she says. 'You should write it up at school.'

'It's not a story,' I yell. 'It's true.'

'Come on,' says Mum. 'Get real. We all know you

have a good imagination. But really.'

'I can prove it,' I yell.

I run into the bedroom to get the six spare fingers.

But they're gone. A breeze blows gently through the open window. I poke my head out of the window. There's no one there. Not even Slurp.

So that's that. Mum doesn't believe me. No new fingers grow on my hands. Thank goodness.

Everything goes back to normal.

Except for one or two things. Gumble stays well away from me. He never puts a finger up at me again.

Slurp is different too. She bites at people's fingers when they pat her. She seems to like the taste. And she grows new ears. But they don't last for long because she keeps scratching them off. And they get eaten by the dog next-door – the big mongrel with the long tail.

Round the Bend

THUMP.

'Oh, gawd,' said my friend Derek.

'What?'

'We've run over a dog.'

Derek's dad looked in the mirror and pulled the Mercedes over to the side of the road. The three of us jumped out and started walking back to the small, still bundle in the middle of the road.

'Don't worry,' said Derek. 'My dad will take care of things.'

We were on our way to a volleyball game. Derek's dad was taking a shortcut because we were late.

It was dark and hard to see. But the dog seemed to be lying very still. I didn't want to look. What if it was dead and all squashed, with blood and guts hanging out? Or even worse – what if it was squashed and alive? What would we do then?

I could feel my stomach churning. I rushed over to a bush and threw up. The spew splashed all over my shoes. Ugh. I hate being sick. And I hate looking like a wimp.

Derek's dad had already reached the dog. He was bending down, trying to see in the dark. Before he could move, a feeble voice filtered through the trees. 'Tinker, Tinker. Come here, boy. Where are you?'

A little old man with wispy hair stumbled onto the road. 'Have you seen –' he started to say. His gaze fell on the small dog lying on the road. 'Tinker?' he said. He fell to his knees with a sob and started to feel all over the dog. He tried to find a pulse.

'Gone,' he said looking up at us as if we were murderers. 'Our poor little Tinker.'

We all stared guiltily at each other. I didn't know what to say. Derek and I walked over to the dog. It was very dark but I could see a little smear of blood coming out of one nostril. The dog was a bit flat and stiff. But that was all. No bones sticking out or anything awful like that. If it wasn't for the glassy, staring eyes you might have thought it was still alive.

The old man clasped the dog to his chest as if it was a baby. Then he stumbled off towards a nearby farmhouse without another word.

I wanted to get back in the car and drive off. I just wanted to put a big distance between us and what we had done. But not Derek's dad. He was so calm. He always knew what to do. He was a pilot in the airforce. He flew Phantom jets. Once he had to bail out over Bass Strait when an engine caught fire. He was a hero. Strong and handsome and tough.

Just the opposite of my dad. Don't get me wrong. I love my dad. But ... well, let's face it. He's no oil painting. And he drives a beat-up old truck. And he's not a pilot. He's a ...

I just couldn't bring myself to say it. Derek was always asking me what my dad does. I didn't want to tell him. It was too awful.

Derek's dad stared up the track. What was he going to do? Jump in the car and drive off? No way. 'Listen, boys,' he said. 'We have to do the right thing. We have to try and make up for what we've done.'

'Dad always does the right thing,' said Derek proudly.

A light was shining on the porch of the small farmhouse. Derek's dad started to walk towards it. We followed along behind. I had a sinking feeling in my stomach. And it wasn't because I'd just been sick.

The old man might not be very pleased to see us. He might go troppo.

But then I cheered up. After all, Derek's dad had parachuted out of a jet fighter at ten thousand metres. He could handle anything.

2

Derek's dad knocked on the farmhouse door. Not a little timid knock like my dad would have done. A real loud, confident knock. Derek smiled.

There was a bit of shuffling and rustling inside and then the door swung open. I could just make out the shape of the dog covered by a blanket in front of the fire inside. The old man stared at us with tear-filled eyes. His lips started to tremble. For a minute I thought he was going to faint.

'The dog just ran out of nowhere,' said Derek's dad. 'We didn't even see it.'

'Tinker,' said the old man. 'Poor darling Tinker.'

'We'd like to do something,' said Derek's dad. 'I know how you must feel.'

The old man beckoned us inside. Derek's dad gave us a confident nod and led the way. The room was gloomy, lit only by a lamp. The old man collapsed into a chair and sank his head into his hands. He started to sob and rub at his eyes. Then he looked up and spoke.

'Please excuse me,' he said. 'I'm not crying for me. I'm crying for Jason.'

'Jason?' said Derek's dad.

The old man held a finger to his lips. Then he hobbled across the room and silently opened a door. We tiptoed over and peeped in. A small boy with a pale face was sleeping peacefully in a rough wooden bed.

'My grandson, Jason,' said the old man. 'His parents were both killed in a car accident last year. He wouldn't talk to anyone. Not a word. Just sat looking at the wall. Until I bought him that dog. As a puppy. It got him talking again. "Tinker," he said. "I'll call him Tinker."'

A tear started to run down the old man's cheek.

We all fell silent and stared at Jason lying there asleep. The poor kid. His parents were dead. And now his dog, Tinker, was dead too. What would he say when he woke up? Would he lose his speech again?

Derek's dad pulled out his wallet. 'I'll pay for a new dog,' he said.

'Good on ya, Dad,' said Derek. His dad was so kind. He couldn't bring Tinker back to life but he was going to pay for a replacement. We all stared at the wallet. It was stuffed full of money. That was another good thing about Derek's dad. He was rich.

The old man shook his head. 'He won't take to a new dog,' he said. 'It'll have to be Tinker or nothing.'

Derek's dad shook his head sadly. 'I can't bring Tinker back from the dead,' he said. 'No one can do that. But where did you get the dog?'

The old man brightened up a bit. 'Fish Creek,' he said. 'There's a guy down there who breeds them.'

3

We spent ages driving around country back roads. In the middle of the night. Looking for the kennels at Fish Creek where the dead dog came from. 'We'll never find it,' I groaned.

Derek's dad stopped the car at a dark crossroads. 'Get out, boys,' he said.

We scrambled out of the car and stood there in the silent countryside. Derek and I didn't have a clue what was going on.

'Listen,' said Derek's dad.

We listened. We strained our ears. Nothing but crickets and frogs. But then. Then. Faintly. Far away. The sound of dogs barking. We all grinned. Derek's dad was so smart.

'You're a genius, Dad,' said Derek.

I thought about my own dad. He would be at the volleyball match. He'd gone on ahead. On his own. He knew I wanted to have a ride in the Mercedes. He didn't mind having no one to talk to. My dad was a quiet person.

Derek's dad followed the sound of the dogs until we came to the kennels. It was a ratty old place with cages and dumped cars everywhere. As we drew up to the house dozens of dogs began to snarl and snap and howl. I was glad they were in cages. They sounded like they wanted to tear us to pieces.

A big guy in a blue singlet staggered out and looked into the car. He had a bushy beard. In one hand he held a stubby of beer. Over on the porch I saw a speedboat. A brand-new one by the look of it.

'Nick off,' growled the guy in the blue singlet. 'We don't like strangers in the middle of the night.'

Derek's dad opened his wallet. 'We've come to buy a dog,' he said.

'Yeah,' said Derek.

The bloke grinned with big yellow teeth and opened the car door. 'In that case,' he said. 'Come in.'

Derek's dad told him the story of little Jason and the dead dog and how we wanted another one the same before he woke up.

'Only one left from the litter,' said the dog breeder. 'And I can't remember if it looks the same as Tinker.' He led us out to a shed and showed us a dog. We all smiled at each other. It was exactly the same as the dead dog. It even had a little brown patch on its left ear.

'Just the shot,' beamed Derek's dad. 'How much?'

'A thousand dollars.'

Derek's dad turned pale. 'How much?' he said again.

'A thousand bucks,' said the dog breeder. 'This is my breeding bitch. It's the only female in the country. They are very rare dogs. Mongolian Rat Catchers.'

'You can afford it, Dad,' said Derek. 'Go on, buy it.'

Derek's dad looked at us. He looked at the dog breeder. He looked at the dog. Then he handed over the thousand dollars. In cash.

What a man. Fancy paying a thousand dollars. Just to help out a little boy he didn't even know.

'My father doesn't even have a thousand dollars,' I thought to myself. 'Geez, Derek is lucky.'

4

'Let's go,' said Derek's dad. 'We have to get back with this dog before little Jason wakes up and finds out that Tinker is dead.'

We jumped into the Mercedes and tore back to the farmhouse. The little man opened the door before we could even knock. 'He's still asleep,' he whispered. 'Come in quick.'

We all walked into the gloomy room and Derek's dad put the new dog on the table. It immediately started to lick the little man's hand. He peered at it carefully and then wiped tears of joy from his eyes. 'Amazing,' he said. 'It's exactly the same. Jason will never know the difference.'

The new dog wagged its tail happily.

'Where's the dead dog?' asked Derek's dad.

The little man picked up a sack and opened it. We all stared into the gloom at the dead dog. There was no doubt about it. You just couldn't tell the difference between the two animals.

The new dog jumped off the table, ran over to the sack and started barking like crazy. It didn't like what was in there at all. The noise was enough to wake the dead. 'Tinker, Tinker?' came a boy's weak voice. The old man threw a quick look at little Jason's door and quickly pushed the sack aside. Then he grabbed the new dog and took it into the bedroom.

We all followed him into the room. Jason was sitting up in bed, calling to the new dog feebly. He looked at it. He frowned. He looked puzzled. 'Tinker,' he said in a worried voice. 'You've lost your collar.'

The old man shuffled back into the kitchen, put his hand into the sack and took the collar from the dead dog. 'Here it is,' he said. 'I was just cleaning it.'

Jason threw out his arms and hugged the new dog. 'Oh Tinker,' he said. 'I love you.'

5

The Mercedes wound it way through the mountains. Now we were really late for the volleyball match. 'It was worth a thousand dollars,' said Derek's dad. 'Just to see the look on that poor boy's face.' Derek and

I smiled at each other. What a man he was. Always so calm.

'You're the greatest, Dad,' said Derek. He looked at me to see if I was going to disagree. I didn't.

When we got to the volleyball stadium my own dad was not calm.

'Where have you been?' he growled. 'The game's over. I thought you must have been in an accident. I was just about to call the police.'

'Calm down, old boy,' said Derek's dad. 'We've got quite a story to tell you.'

Dad listened to the whole thing in silence. He didn't seem impressed.

'Mongolian Rat Catcher,' he said grumpily. 'Never heard of them.'

'Know about dogs, do you?' said Derek's dad. 'Work with animals, do you?'

Dad looked annoyed. He opened his mouth to tell them what he does but I got in first. 'Er, we'd better be going,' I said.

Dad drove back down the mountain. Fast. He asked me a lot of questions about Jason and the dog breeder and the old man. But he didn't say much. He was in a grumpy mood. Why couldn't he be cool? Like Derek's dad.

'It's up here,' I said. 'The place where we hit the dog. Just round the bend.'

Dad dropped down a gear and planted his foot. He roared round the corner really fast. Boy, he was in a bad mood.

THUMP.

'Aaagh,' I screamed.

'What?'

'We've run over a dog.'

Dad looked in the mirror and pulled the truck over to the side of the road. The two of us jumped out and started walking back to the small, still bundle in the middle of the road.

My heart jumped up into my mouth. I felt faint. I felt sick. Dad had run over Jason's new dog. And killed it. I just couldn't believe it. The same thing had happened. Twice. In the same night. But now it was Dad who had killed the dog.

And there was no way he was going to be able to fix things up. He didn't have a thousand dollars. And anyway, there were no more Mongolian Rat Catchers left. We couldn't pull the same trick again.

Dad bent over and looked at the dead dog carefully.

Before he could move, a trembling voice filtered

through the trees. 'Tinker, Tinker. Come here, boy. Where are you?'

The little old man with the wispy hair stumbled onto the road. 'Have you seen –' he started to say. His gaze fell on the small dog lying on the road. 'Tinker?' He said. He fell to his knees with a sob and started to feel all over the dog. His fingers felt for a pulse.

'Gone,' he said looking up at us as if we were murderers. Then his eyes opened wide as he recognised me. 'You've killed two dogs in the same night,' he gasped.

The old man clasped the dog to his chest as if it was a baby. Then he stumbled off towards the nearby farmhouse without another word. Just like he'd done before.

'Hey,' shouted Dad. 'Come back here.'

Why couldn't my dad be more kind and generous? Like Derek's dad. My dad didn't even seem sorry for what he had done. The little man stopped and Dad went towards him.

'Go back to the truck,' Dad growled at me.

I did. I was glad to go back to the truck. I didn't want to see that look in the old man's eyes. I didn't want to hear Jason start crying when he saw the dead dog.

After about ten minutes Dad came back to the truck. He had the dead dog with him. He threw the body onto the back of the truck and started up the engine. 'Show me how to get to the dog kennels,' he said.

'It's no good,' I yelled. 'There are no more Mongolian Rat Catchers left. It was the last one.'

'Just show me the way,' said Dad.

We drove in silence. Except for when I had to point out which way to turn. Why wouldn't Dad listen to me? Why did he have to go back to the dog breeder's place? It was crazy.

6

Finally, we reached the dog kennels. The dogs started up howling and barking just like before. Dad didn't even wait for the dog breeder to come out. He jumped out of the truck and ran up to the door. I saw it open and Dad disappeared inside.

There was a lot of yelling and shouting. What was going on? Should I go and help? Just then the door flew open and Dad came out. He angrily shoved his wallet into his pocket and strode across to our old truck.

Dad didn't have a new dog for little Jason. He didn't even have the dead dog. He was dogless. And he wasn't in the mood for talking.

Neither was I. Why couldn't my dad be calm and cool and rich? Why couldn't my dad have a wallet full of money to buy a new dog for Jason? Why did we have to drive around in a beat-up old truck and not a Mercedes? Why, why, why?

After a long drive we got back to town. Dad stopped outside the front gate.

Of Derek's house.

'What are we doing here?' I said. 'They're probably in bed.'

Dad gave me a big smile. He ruffled my hair in a friendly way. 'Come on, Ned,' he said. 'I don't think they'll mind.'

Derek's dad threw open the front door and stared at us. So did Derek.

'Hello, old boy,' said Derek's dad. 'What's up?'

Dad took out his wallet.

'Oh, no,' I thought. 'He's going to ask Derek's dad for money.'

But he didn't. Dad took out a great wad of notes. 'Here's your thousand dollars back,' he said.

I stared. Derek stared. We all stared.

Dad smiled. 'Tinker was dead all right,' he said. 'A stuffed dead dog. With glass eyes. The little man threw it under every car that passed. Then he sent the guilty driver off to buy the other dog. That dog breeder has sold his Mongolian Rat Catcher to at least fifty suckers.'

Derek's dad took his money back and stood there with his jaw hanging open. 'How did you know?' he stammered.

I looked at Derek and decided to answer the question myself. I was so happy.

'He's a taxidermist,' I said proudly.

Seeshell

'The way I see it,' says Jacko.

'You're pretty small,' says Johnno.

'For a boy of fifteen,' says Tommo.

I look up at the three brothers. They are all wearing the same checked shirts. They all have the same tattoo on the backs of their hands. They are all real big guys. And they are right – I am small for my age.

'Geez,' I think to myself. 'I can hardly tell them apart. They even look like each other.'

I am very nervous. This is my first job ever and I want to do well. All my life I have dreamed about working on a fishing boat like this one. All my life I have wanted to get away and sail out on the open sea. It is only a holiday job but it is my big chance. If I do well the brothers might keep me on for good.

'Come aboard the *Oracle*,' says Jacko.

'And see if you like it,' says Johnno.

'Living on a cray boat,' says Tommo.

I follow the brothers up the gangplank and onto the deck. I breathe in deep. I take in the smell of the salt air and the coiled ropes and the scrubbed decks. 'Ah,' I say out loud. 'Excellent.'

The brothers grin.

'That is a very good sign, Alan,' says Jacko.

'That you are going to do much better . . .' says Johnno.

'Than the last boy,' says Tommo.

I stare up at them. 'What happened to him?' I say.

The three brothers look down into the dark, still water. The smiles fall from their faces. They all speak together. 'He is feeding the fishes,' they say with one angry voice.

I suddenly feel cold all over. A picture comes into my mind. A picture of a silent body lying still on the bottom of the ocean. Fishes nibbling at its toes.

I want to ask, 'What happened? Did he fall overboard?'. But I look into the brothers' brooding eyes and decide not to.

2

The brothers give me jobs straight away. Scrubbing the deck. Stacking the empty craypots. Scraping rust from steel railings and painting them with red undercoat. I am so happy to be going to sea. And so are the brothers. They sing together as they work.

They seem to love one particular song. They sing it over and over. It's about some old guy who lives on a mountain with his daughter. And no one is allowed to go near her. Lots of guys want to because she has lips that are sweeter than honey. But everyone is too scared to risk it because the old guy is handy with a gun and a knife.

The way the brothers lift their voices makes it seem as if they know the person in the song. Sometimes tears come to their eyes as they sing about her tender lips.

Finally I just have to ask. I point to their tattoos and the word that is etched on each hand. 'Who is Shelley?' I ask. 'Is she your mother?'

The brothers stop work.

'She is our sun,' says Jacko.

'She is the stars,' says Johnno.

'She is our little sister,' says Tommo.

'And here she is,' says a soft voice.

I look up and see a girl. She is about my age and very pretty. She wears denim shorts all frayed at the edges. And a tight top. She has deep brown eyes and dark hair. And her feet are bare.

She smiles with a soft, kind mouth. A very nice thought about her tender lips comes into my mind. I try to push it away and stare at the distant cliffs. For a second the rocks at the end of the cliffs seem like two faces kissing. I rub my eyes and turn back to the brothers.

'This is Shelley,' says Jacko.

'If anyone ever touches her,' says Johnno.

'They will end up feeding the fishes like the last kid,' says Tommo.

Shelley gives me a warm smile and holds out her hand. 'Hello,' she says. 'Don't take any notice of them. They don't really mean it.'

I look at the three brothers and can tell that they do really mean it. But I hold out my hand and try very hard not to think about how I would like to kiss Shelley. I try very hard indeed. I do not want to get the sack before I have even started. And I do not want to end up feeding the fishes either.

3

So the cray boat puts out to sea. With me and the brothers and Shelley. I love the work. I learn to put the chopped fish-heads and bones into the craypots for bait. I learn how to lower them down to the bottom of the ocean. How to attach them to buoys so that we can come back and recover the pots. I learn to empty the live crayfish into the holding tank down below. I learn to cook. And scrub. And to keep away from Shelley.

She is on my mind all the time. But every time I get anywhere near her one of the brothers pops up from nowhere and sends me to the other side of the boat.

Not that I would have a chance with someone like her. Beautiful and clever. Not like me. Nah, she wouldn't be interested in me. And even if she was I couldn't risk it. Those brothers mean it. They really would toss me overboard if I so much as touched her.

So I put all my thoughts into my work. I come to love that boat. It is much more than a place of work. It is a home that goes everywhere with us. The sound of the engine turning is like a heart beating. It is almost as if the boat is alive. A friend that will never let me down.

'You are doing well,' says Jacko. 'But –'

'Don't love a boat too much,' says Johnno.

'It is only a boat,' says Tommo. 'It can't love you back.'

But I am not too sure. Sometimes at night when the moonlight is on the water and the sea is still, the boat seems to talk to me. I think I was born to go to sea.

4

One morning, early, I watch Johnno pulling in a craypot. It is deep in the green sea, somewhere out of sight. I watch the dark shape gradually take form as it nears the surface. Closer and closer. There is something in it but it is not a crayfish.

Johnno dumps the craypot on the deck. Then he gives a terrible scream. 'Aagh. Seeshell,' he yells. 'Seeshell.'

Jacko and Tommo scramble over to the pot as fast as they can go.

I look at the shell. It is a creamy colour, rippled and shaped like a beautiful clam. It is tightly shut.

The brothers are staring at the Seeshell as if it is a hand grenade that is about to go off.

Tommo races into the cabin and comes out with a pair of barbecue tongs. 'Shut your eyes,' he screams. 'Shut your eyes.' He lifts out the Seeshell very gently. His hands are shaking and I can see that he is scared.

Johnno has his eyes tightly shut. 'Careful,' he whispers.

Jacko has his hands over his eyes. 'Don't drop it,' he says. 'It might open.'

Tommo holds the Seeshell out over the water and lets go. *Plink*, it splashes into the ocean and swirls down into the depths.

The brothers start to race around like crazy. 'Lift the anchor,' yells Johnno. 'This is a bad spot for fishing.'

'Pull in the other craypot, Alan,' shouts Jacko.

Tommo disappears into the wheelhouse and starts the engine. The brothers sure are in a terrible hurry to get out of here. Shelley is down below. She doesn't know anything about what's been going on.

I start to pull up the rope on the other craypot. Faster and faster. Here it comes. There is something in it. A crayfish? A crab? What is it?

The brothers are all getting the boat ready to leave.

Shelley is pulling in the anchor with the electric winch. Nobody is taking any notice of me.

I grab the craypot and haul it onto the deck. Then I look inside.

5

It is a Seeshell. Much smaller than the other one. It is also creamy and rippled. But one thing is different. The shell is starting to open and strange red tentacles wave like slippery eyelashes. I give a shudder and open my mouth to yell out to the brothers.

But then it happens. Oh, weird. Disgusting. Oh, yuck.

The shell opens right up and there inside is something looking out. An eye. Right in the middle is a bulging eye. Not a fish-type eye, cold and still. But a human-type eye with a pupil.

The eye stares at me.

And I stare back.

I start to think. All my life I have been poor. I have never had expensive Christmas presents. I have never even owned a bike.

And now I am staring at a fortune. A shell with an eye? No one has ever seen such a thing. I could sell it. The story would be worth millions. Newspapers, magazines, television, the Internet. Everyone would want to see it. But for some reason the brothers do not want to keep the Seeshell. They are scared of it. Maybe they are superstitious.

If I show the Seeshell to the brothers, I already know what they will do. They will throw it back. But at the moment they are too busy getting the boat ready to leave. They are not paying any attention to me.

I see an old bait jar nearby. As quick as lightning I tip the contents into the sea. Then I grab the tongs that Tommo had thrown on the deck. With shaking fingers I drop the Seeshell into the jar and screw on the lid. The Seeshell closes up as tight as a clam. For the moment the eye is gone from sight.

I carefully hide the jar under some ropes and get on with my jobs. After a couple of hours the brothers stop the boat.

'This is a much better spot,' says Jacko. 'We'll put down the pots.'

So that is what we do.

Dropping pots is slow work and it takes half a day to lower them down into the water. We attach a rope to each craypot and leave a buoy so that we can find it again. All the time I am working I can only think of two things. The eye in the Seeshell, and Shelley, the brothers' beautiful sister.

Shelley seems to want to talk to me but I am scared to go near her. Once my hand accidentally touched hers when we were cleaning fish. It sent a tingle right up my arm.

But I can't think about it. It is too dangerous. I get stuck into my jobs and try to forget about her. Finally I am finished. I grab the bait jar and then go to my favourite spot at the back of the boat. This part of the boat is low and I can touch the sea with my hand. I take the lid off the jar and fill it up with salt water. I don't want the Seeshell to die. It won't be worth as much if it dies.

I screw the lid back on the jar and watch. The Seeshell slowly opens. There it is. There is the eye. It stares at me without blinking.

Suddenly I see something weird. Not in the jar. Not on the boat. Not out to sea. Not even in the sky.

What I see is inside my head. A picture inside my mind. Just as clear as day. It's as if I am watching a movie. I see a little scene that is not really happening. I see Johnno coming up from below. He hauls himself up onto the deck, leans over the side and spits into the water. Then he wipes his forehead with his arm. Even when I close my eyes I can still see him doing it.

I open my eyes and see that the Seeshell has closed. There is no one else on the deck. My brain seems to freeze over. What is going on? Am I seeing things? Am I going crazy? Having visions about things that are not really there.

Suddenly I hear something from below. Someone is coming. I quickly shove the Seeshell jar under some ropes. I hear footsteps. Johnno hauls himself up onto the deck, leans over the side and spits into the water. Then he wipes his forehead with his arm.

Just like he did in my vision.

I saw him do that. I saw him spit into the water before he even did it. Something is terribly wrong with me. I need help.

But who can I ask? Johnno and Tommo and Jacko will be mad at me for keeping the Seeshell. I might end up feeding the fishes like the last kid. Is that what he did wrong? Kept a Seeshell when he wasn't supposed to?

What will I do?

6

'Okay,' says Johnno. 'Let's get going.'

'Let's find a place to anchor,' says Tommo.

'For the night,' says Jacko.

Tommo starts the engine and we head for shore.

There is nothing for me to do so I sit up the back of the boat and think.

I go over and over what happened. And it all comes down to this. When I looked into the eye of the Seeshell I saw something before it happened. I saw Johnno spit into the water before he did it.

Yes. There is no doubt about it. The Seeshell can see into the future. It knows what is going to happen. And it can send out thoughts. It can make *me* see what is going to happen too.

The sun sinks into the ocean and soft moonlight floats on the gently swelling sea. The jar with the Seeshell inside is out of sight under the ropes. I know what I should do. I should grab the jar and throw it into the ocean. Johnno and Tommo and Jacko don't like it. Seeshells are dangerous. I should never look at it again.

But then I think about it. It would be great to see into the future. You could win bets. You could tell someone's fortune. You would know what lotto numbers were coming up. You could win first prize every time.

I look into the jar. The Seeshell seems to be calling to me. It wants me to pick it up. 'Come here,' it seems to say. 'Fall under my spell.'

Is it the Seeshell speaking? Or are these my own thoughts?

Slowly, slowly, slowly, I reach under the ropes and pull out the jar. The Seeshell is tightly closed. It is keeping all of its secrets to itself.

Then suddenly it starts to open. It reminds me of a mouth yawning. And there it is. The terrible eye. Staring at me.

I shudder and shut my own eyes. Straight away I see another vision. I see a picture in my head. As clear as day. Only it is not day. It is night, and soft moonlight is floating gently on the swelling sea.

In my vision the *Oracle* is cutting through the water at high speed. It is heading straight for a reef of jagged rocks just above the surface of the water. In the moonlight I can plainly see the edges of a cruel reef. *Crunch*. The *Oracle* runs straight into the rocks. A terrible hole is torn into the bow just above the waterline.

I open my eyes in horror. The Seeshell has shown me what is going to happen. We are going to smash into a reef and damage the boat. And I am the only one who knows it.

Think, think, think. Yes, I know what to do. Yes, I know. I will make Johnno change course. Then we won't crash into the waiting rocks that lie out there in the night. We will go a different way. We will be saved.

But how can I make Johnno change course?

Simple.

'Rocks,' I yell. 'Rocks dead ahead.'

Johnno puts his head out of the wheelhouse. 'I can't see them,' he yells.

'Straight ahead,' I yell. 'Change course.'

Johnno shouts back in a hoarse voice. 'We're on course. We're in the channel. I've been here a thousand times. There are no rocks in the channel.'

He is not going to change course. And the Seeshell has shown me what lies ahead. I have to do something.

'I see them,' I yell. 'I see rocks.'

Johnno pulls fiercely on the wheel. The boat changes direction.

I have done it. I have put us on a different course. Now the Seeshell's prophecy will not come true.

Oh, it is so good to be able to see into the future.

The *Oracle* is cutting through the water at high speed. The empty sea is . . .

Not empty.

The boat is heading straight for a reef of jagged rocks just above the surface of the water. In the moonlight I can plainly see the edges of a cruel reef.

Crunch.

The *Oracle* runs straight into the rocks. A terrible hole is torn into the bow just above the waterline.

7

The brothers run to the front and stare at the hole. We are not in danger but the boat has been badly damaged. Johnno is furious. 'You mongrel. You led us onto the rocks,' he screamed. 'Look what you have done.'

He grabs my head and shoves it over the side. He wants me to look but I can't. The hole in the boat is like a gash in living flesh. A wound inflicted on a friend. I can't believe what has happened. The Seeshell showed me the boat crashing onto rocks. I tried to stop it. But my actions made it happen. There is no way to stop the future. Once the Seeshell shows you something you can't stop it happening.

Now I know why the brothers are scared of the Seeshell. Now I know why they moved to another fishing ground when they caught one. Seeshells are bad news.

There is only one thing left to do. I have to get rid of the Seeshell. And quick.

The brothers are pulling a cover over the hole in the bow. They ignore me. I am in disgrace. I make my way to the back of the boat and carefully take out the jar. It is dark and I can't see the Seeshell. Good. I am safe from it.

Oh, no, no, no. The moon comes out. And there in its silvery light I can see the eye of the Seeshell glaring up at me.

And I see something else. A vision. Inside my head. As clear as day I see the faces of the brothers. Watching something. Scowling. Angry. Creeping forward. And then I see what they are looking at. They are looking at me. And what I am doing.

Shelley and I are kissing.

Suddenly the Seeshell closes its eye and the vision is gone. The moon is still shining.

A sentence comes into my mind. A single sentence. A death sentence. The words ring in my head. *Feeding the fishes.* The brothers will catch me and throw me over the side. I will end up like the last boy on the *Oracle*.

But then I stop and think. I don't have to kiss her. It is up to me. The Seeshell can't make you do things. It can only show you what is going to happen.

Okay, so Shelley is beautiful. I can't stop thinking about her. But I don't have to kiss her, do I? It is up to me. I am in charge of what I do. I am not so love-crazed that I can't stop myself from kissing her.

But just to be on the safe side I will keep the Seeshell a little longer. Just in case. After all, the brothers are still mad at me. It could be useful to know what is going to happen.

Morning comes.

'Get below,' growls Johnno. 'And help Shelley cook breakfast. We are going to repair the damage to the bow.'

He is in a really bad mood, I can see that. So I hot-foot it down to the galley as quick as I can.

Shelley gives me a warm smile. 'You make the toast,' she says. 'While I fry the eggs.'

Oh, she is a beautiful girl. And kind. She is everything a guy could want. Would I like to kiss

55

her? Oh, would I? There is nothing in the world that I would like better.

But I am not going to. No way. Nothing can make me kiss her.

Firstly because I would never kiss a girl unless she wanted me to. And secondly because the brothers will kill me if I do.

So I am safe.

But I am also not concentrating on what I am doing.

'Look out,' yells Shelley.

Black smoke is pouring out of the toaster. The bread is burning. Shelley and I both run for it at the same time. *Crash*. We bump into each other and Shelley starts to fall. I grab her and just stop her from slipping.

Her eyes look into mine and we both laugh.

If ever I was going to kiss her it would be now. But I am not going to. No way. I am not going to end up feeding the fishes. There is nothing in the world that can make me kiss that girl.

So I don't.

But something does happen. Something I cannot stop. Something that is not my fault.

Shelley speaks to me in a trembling voice. 'I have

been wanting to do this since the first time I saw you, Alan,' she says.

She pulls my head towards her and before I know what is happening she kisses me full on the lips.

She kisses *me*. No, no, no, no, no. I can't believe it.

And worse. So much worse. Through the swirling smoke I see the brothers. Coming towards me with fists bunched.

8

This is serious. I have to get away. And fast. I clamber up the emergency ladder and escape through a hatch.

I hear loud angry voices coming from below.

'Grab the little devil,' yells Jacko.

'After him quick,' yells Johnno.

'He kissed our sister,' yells Tommo.

I stare around the deck. Where can I run? Where can I go? What is going to happen?

There is one way to find out. I grab the jar and stare inside but the Seeshell is closed. Its shell is tightly shut. There is no eye in sight. I give the jar a shake. 'Wake up,' I yell. 'Wake up.'

The shell slowly opens and there it is. The terrible

eye. Staring at me. Silent, unblinking. Staring into the future.

Straight away I see a vision. I see myself lying on the deck. I see my hands tied behind my back. My feet are lashed together. I am shouting something but I don't know what. I see the brothers lift up my struggling body. I see Shelley, locked in the cabin nearby, crying. The tears are running down her face. I see the brothers throw my struggling body over the side. I see myself sink beneath the waves. Gone to feed the fishes.

I am history. All of this is going to happen and there is nothing I can do about it.

'Get him,' says a voice. It is Johnno.

The brothers have found me.

'Grab him,' says Jacko.

'Quick,' says Johnno.

'Stop him,' says Tommo.

But they cannot stop me. I am already climbing up the mast. Up, up, up.

The deck is far below. The ship is swaying from side to side in a strong swell. It is a long way down. I am scared. And I feel sick. I hate heights. In my trembling hands I hold the jar. And in the jar is the terrible Seeshell. I cannot hold on to the mast and the jar at the same time. I need both hands. Suddenly the jar slips from my fingers. Over and over it spins and then – *smash*.

The jar breaks into a billion pieces on the deck.

For a second the brothers stare. Then they start to scream and yell. 'Aagh. A Seeshell. Get rid of it. Quick. Don't look. It's opening. Don't look. Don't look.' The brothers hold their hands over their eyes. They turn their backs on the Seeshell. They are terrified of it.

Johnno falls down on his hands and knees. He has his eyes tightly closed. He starts to crawl forward, feeling his way like a blind dog. He feels around with his hands.

Touching this. Touching that. But not touching the thing he is after. The awesome, the all-knowing Seeshell. It is starting to open.

Closer and closer. He dabs at the deck with his fingers. Each time just missing the shell. Finally he finds it. Without opening his eyes he forces the Seeshell closed and throws it into the air. It cuts a wide arc above the boat. *Plink*. It is gone. Back where it came from. Into the ocean.

The brothers open their eyes and look up at me.

'So,' says Johnno.

'You looked at a Seeshell,' says Tommo.

'And now you know what you don't want to know,' says Jacko.

'I know what you are going to do,' I yell.

'You kissed our little sister,' yells Tommo angrily.

'No one gets away with that,' says Johnno.

'No one at all,' says Jacko.

Suddenly there is another voice speaking. A kind voice. But an angry voice. It is Shelley.

'He did not kiss me,' she says.

'We saw him,' the three brothers say in one voice.

'You did not see him kiss me,' she says. 'You saw *me* kiss *him*.'

The brothers look at each other. For once they do not know what to say.

'Come down, boy,' says Johnno at last.

I shake my head. He still sounds furious. He is still mad at me. 'No way,' I say. 'The Seeshell showed me what you are going to do. I know you are going to throw me over the side.'

'Then you also know . . .' says Jacko.

'That nothing can stop us doing it,' says Johnno.

'So you might as well come down and get it over with,' says Tommo.

9

So here I am. Lying on the deck. My hands tied behind my back. My feet lashed together. I am shouting something. 'Head first,' I yell. 'Head first.' I see the brothers lift up my struggling body. I see Shelley, locked in the cabin nearby, crying. The tears are running down her face. 'More,' I yell. 'More tears.'

I see the brothers throw my struggling body over the side. I sink beneath the waves.

Gone to feed the fishes?

No. I undo the quick-release knots on my hands and ankles. I float quickly up to the surface. Johnno is waiting there with an outstretched hand. So is Shelley. She is laughing and happy.

Johnno pulls me into the boat and gives me a towel. 'It worked,' he says. 'We acted your vision out perfectly. You can't stop the Seeshell's prophecy from coming true. But you can *make* it come true in your own way.'

I grin at the three brothers. It was a good plan. We acted out what the Seeshell saw. But we added our own little bit at the end. I undid the knots and escaped.

And Shelley cried really convincing fake tears.

The brothers helped me. They are not murderers after all. Or are they? I frown and start to worry.

'What's up?' says Johnno. 'What's wrong now?'

'You are still killers,' I say slowly. 'What about the first boy? What about him?'

'We sacked him. He got another job,' says Jacko.

'But they are not going to sack you,' says Shelley firmly.

'How could he get another job?' I yell. 'You said he's feeding the fishes.'

'He is,' says Jacko.

'Definitely feeding the fishes,' says Johnno.

'He works in an aquarium,' says Tommo.

Piddler on the Roof

Dad and I were having a pee in the garden. Dad stood there staring at the moon and listening to the soft splash of wee on the grass. 'Poetry,' he said. 'It's the only word for taking a leak in your own backyard.'

I unzipped my fly. 'Magic,' I said.

Mum thought it was disgusting but there was nothing she could do about it. Dad said that Man had been standing in the forest peeing on the plants since the dawn of time. He had a speech all worked out about nature and Ancient Man sitting around the campfire.

'It's only natural,' he would say, 'for a man to get out and watch the stars . . .'

'Twinkle,' I would yell.

Then we would both start to laugh like crazy.

Every time it was the same old joke about the stars twinkling but we always thought it was funny. My dad was a great bloke. And we were great mates.

So there we were, standing side by side. Watering the lawn.

'Swordfight,' I yelled.

'You're on, sport,' said Dad.

Our two streams of pee crossed each other in the darkness like two watery blades fighting it out in times of old. Usually I ran out of ammo first and Dad would win. But tonight I beat him easily.

'Well done, Weesle,' said Dad. 'You're amazing. You could beat a horse.'

I blushed with pride and grinned as we walked back to the house. I remembered the time when the kids at school treated me like a little squirt. But that was long ago, before I proved myself in the great peeing competition.

Now life was really good.

But not for long.

2

'Look at this,' said Mum. Her eyes were glued to the television as she spoke. 'The tap water has got bugs in it. It's been contaminated. No one in the whole of Sydney can drink our water.'

'We'll have to drink Coke,' I said hopefully.

'Bottled water,' said Mum. 'They're selling it in all the shops.'

'We won't be able to have a shower,' I said even more hopefully.

'You can wash in it,' said Mum. 'But not drink it. It's disgraceful.'

We stood there listening to the man on the news saying how it was dangerous to drink the water. Especially for old people.

And children.

When he said the last two words I sort of felt funny inside. Mum and Dad were staring at me with a strange look in their eyes.

'Oh, no,' I yelled. 'No you don't. I'm not leaving. I'm not going back to the Outlaws.'

'You know what the doctor told you,' said Dad. 'One more infection and you're gone.'

I smacked my fist into my palm angrily. It was

true. I had a problem with my lungs. If I got infected it was serious.

'Not the Outlaws,' I said. 'Please.'

'I wish you wouldn't call my sister and Ralph "the Outlaws",' said Mum.

'Dad does,' I started to say. He was shaking his head at me. He didn't want me to dob him in. He was the one who started calling Aunty Sue and Ralph the Outlaws. He couldn't stand them either.

'Sorry, mate,' said Dad. 'But you'll have to go to Dingle until the scare is over.'

I stared hopelessly at them both. I decided to save my breath. When they both lined up against me there was no way I could win.

3

The next morning I stepped off the train at Dingle. Horrible Aunty Sue and her even more horrible son, Ralph, were there to meet me.

'Hello, Weesle,' said Ralph in a sickly sweet voice. 'I'm looking forward to this.'

He was too, and I knew why.

'Get in the car, Weesle,' said Aunty Sue. 'We're running late. This visit really is inconvenient. You couldn't have come at a worse time. You'll have to look after yourself. I'm too busy with the hospital fete.

'I'll look after him again,' said Ralph with a sneer.

Aunty Sue smiled at him. 'You are a kind boy,' she said. She picked up my bag and frowned.

'What have you got in here?' she said.

'Bottled water,' I told her.

'You don't need that here, droob,' said Ralph. 'Our water is pure. Not like the stinky stuff in the city.'

'The doctor said I have to,' I told him. 'Just to be on the safe side. But I'm allowed to drink lemonade.'

'No soft drinks,' snapped Aunty Sue. 'Bad for your teeth.'

I secretly felt the ten dollars in my pocket. I could buy my own Coke.

4

Aunty Sue and Ralph lived in a small cottage in the middle of Dingle. My room was up in the roof.

I plonked down my bags and sat on the bed. Ralph closed the door so Aunty Sue couldn't hear. He held out his hand. 'Pay up, Weesle,' he said. 'A dollar a day. Pay the rent.'

Ralph was much bigger than me. And he was a bully. But I shook my head.

'No way,' I said. 'Not this time. You can sneak on me all you like. Last time I stayed ten days. Ten dollars. All my pocket money. I need it to buy Coke. I can't just drink water the whole time.'

Ralph stood up and left. He didn't say a word. He didn't have to. We both knew what he was going to do.

Dob. Rat on me. Tell tales.

Call it what you like. It is the same thing. He was going to tell Aunty Sue every time I did the slightest thing wrong.

And he did. Right away.

Aunty Sue held out her hand. 'Give me the ten dollars, Weesle,' she said. 'Soft drinks are bad for your teeth.'

I handed over the ten dollars with a big sigh. This was going to be a long ten days.

The way it turned out it was a long ten hours. Ralph dobbed me in for the smallest little thing.

'Mum, Weesle didn't wipe his feet.'

'Inconsiderate child,' said Aunty Sue.

'Mum, Weesle didn't clean his teeth.'

'Unhealthy child,' said Aunty Sue.

'Mum, Weesle stole some ice-cream.'

'Thief,' yelled Aunty Sue.

'Mum, Weesle picked his nose.'

'Disgusting child,' sniffed Aunty Sue.

'Mum, Weesle didn't wash his hands before the meal.'

'Filthy boy,' yelled Aunty Sue.

This went on all afternoon. Aunty Sue had a thing about health. You had to have clean finger-nails. You had to wipe your mouth with a napkin after a meal. You had to spray stuff that smelled of flowers around in the toilet. You had to search the plug-hole in the shower for hairs after you had used it.

Aunty Sue was a health freak of the worst sort. And every time I broke a rule Ralph would dob on me.

5

By the time night came I just couldn't take any more. I looked out of my little attic window on the roof and blinked back tears. I wanted to go home.

I wanted to see Mum again. I wanted Dad. I wanted my own messy room.

I looked up at the stars.

I wanted a twinkle.

I was really busting by the time I got outside. Oh, it was lovely to be out there in the backyard at night. It reminded me of Dad and our sword fights. And our conversations about the meaning of life.

I quickly pulled down my fly and let fly.

'Filthy, disgusting, despicable child.' The words broke the peaceful night like a stone thrown through a window. It was Aunty Sue. And Ralph. He had dobbed on me. He knew I liked to take a leak in the garden. And he had told Aunty Sue.

'Get back inside,' she shrieked. 'Get back to your room. And don't leave it. Stay in that room and don't come out. Weesle, you are disgusting. You're going home first thing in the morning.'

I couldn't see Ralph's face. But I knew it had a smirk plastered all over it.

It was agony trying to stop the pee. Trying to stop in mid-piddle is really bad for your health. It is just torture. But I used all of my strength and managed to stop the flow. I pulled up my zip, raced back up to my room and slammed the door.

There was good news and bad news.

The good news was that they were sending me home in the morning. Terrific.

The bad news was that I couldn't leave the room to go to the loo. And I was busting to finish my leak.

There is really nothing worse than needing to have a pee and not being able to.

I knew that if I left the room Ralph would dob.

The minutes ticked by. Then the hours. The pressure built up. The pain was terrible. Unbearable. I rolled around on the bed. I staggered around the room with my knees held together. Finally, I couldn't stand it any longer. I ran to the little attic window and threw it open.

Oh, wonderful, wonderful, wonderful. The yellow stream fizzled out into the night like a burst water main. A beautiful melody. Magic. Music to the ear. Wee on a tin roof is not as good as wee on the grass. But it is still a lovely sound. I smiled as it splashed on the metal and trickled down into the spouting.

6

The next morning Aunty Sue pushed me onto the train. 'Go back to the filthy city and its filthy water,' she said.

'Yeah,' said Ralph. 'Our tank water is pure.'

'Is it?' I said.

Ticker

I hated the wind.

Especially that night.

Oh, yes, the wind. It ripped and tore at Grandad's old house on the edge of the cliff. It was so bad that I hid my head under the pillow to stop the sound of its shrieking. But I was still scared. I could feel the floor trembling. And the water in the glass next to my bed slopped around as if shaken by an invisible hand.

Outside, the sea boiled. Huge waves threw themselves at the cliffs in fury. Salt spray whipped against the windows. Fierce gusts flattened the grass in the paddocks.

'Are you scared, Keith?' said a friendly voice. It was Grandad. He sat down on the bed and took my hand. 'It's only a storm,' he said. 'It will be over soon. Try to go to sleep.'

I felt safe while he was there. But I knew that he would soon go away and then I would be on my own again. So I tried to keep him talking. I pointed to his watch. The one they gave him when he retired from the railways. It was a great watch. I loved it. Made out of solid gold. Dependable. Like Grandad.

'What makes it go?' I asked him. 'Does it have a battery?'

'No,' said Grandad. 'No battery.'

'Do you wind it up?'

'Nope.'

That had me puzzled. If you didn't wind it up and it didn't have batteries, how could it go?

'What then?' I asked.

He waved his arm around. 'When you move it the watch winds itself. The movement of your hand keeps it going.'

'What about when you take it off?' I asked.

'It can go for twelve hours. Then it stops. But you only need eight hours sleep. So you can take it off at night.' He gave my head a bit of a rub. 'And sleep is just what you need,' he said. He stood up, smiled and left me alone.

Well, not alone. Grandad's dog, Sandy, was hiding under my bed. Whimpering. Scared of the storm.

Sandy wasn't supposed to come inside but we always let her when the thunder started. It's funny how dogs that are really brave turn to shaking jelly when it thunders.

A huge gust of wind buffeted the window. For a moment I thought that the glass was going to break and send sharp spears flying into my room. The rain sounded like a million bullets spitting against the pane.

'Shoot,' I said to myself. 'I'm getting out of here.'

I jumped out of bed and ran down to the lounge. Grandad and Grandma were holding hands in the dark. Watching the lightning tear at the sky. They didn't know that I was there. They didn't know that someone was listening.

'Keith was asking about my watch,' said Grandad.

'You should leave it to him,' said Grandma. 'To remember you by.'

Grandad shook his head. 'I want you to have it, Elsie,' he said. 'And I want you to promise me something.'

Grandma turned her wrinkled face towards him. 'Anything,' she said. 'Anything.'

He waved his arm around. 'Look,' he said. 'I want you to keep it going. Keep it ticking. Don't let it stop. When I die I want you to put this watch on. Its tick will remind you that for all those years my heart was beating close to yours. Promise?'

'Promise,' said Grandma. 'I'll wear it always. I won't let it stop. Not until we meet again.'

I just stood there. Frozen. My heart seemed to miss a beat. Tears started to squeeze out of my eyes. I didn't want Grandad to die. Grandads aren't supposed to die. Especially when you don't have a mum or dad.

Grandads are meant to be there forever. Laughing at your jokes. Fixing your bike. Flying kites. Bringing you special presents. Reading you stories in bed. Making you feel better in storms.

Grandma put an arm around Grandad's old, bent shoulders. 'I'll listen to it every day,' she said. 'It's ticking now and I'll keep it going. It will never stop. That's my promise.'

I crept back to my room. Suddenly the storm didn't seem to matter any more. What if the roof tore away? What if the windows blew in? What if the whole house was blasted into the sky? What did that matter?

It didn't matter at all. Not when you knew that one day soon your Grandad might not be there.

I lay there under the covers thinking about it. Not hearing the wind.

When Grandad's heart stopped, Grandma was going to take his watch from his wrist and put it on. She was going to keep it going. It was sort of like keeping him there with her. As if the ticking was his heart still beating.

It was so sad.

2

The next day the wind was still blowing but the storm had gone.

Grandad and I struggled along the edge of the cliff, carrying fishing rods. Gulls flew above, hovering in the uprush of air off the sea. Sandy ran from rabbit hole to rabbit hole, sniffing and snorting. Loving every minute.

'I'm taking you to my special spot,' said Grandad. 'It's a long way and no one knows it except me and Grandma. The best fishing hole on the coast. I want you to keep it a secret. Pass it on in the family after I'm gone.'

'That won't be for a long time, will it?' I said.

Grandad didn't seem to hear. He just smiled and

changed the subject. 'Here's Fred's Bridge,' he said.

I gasped at the sight. It was one of those cable bridges that are built on two ropes. It stretched high above a gorge. Way down below, the sea was sucking and swelling over black rocks. Every now and then a tremendous wave would thunder into the gorge and send salt spray shooting up almost to the top.

I didn't like the look of it. Not one bit. If there was one thing worse than the wind it was heights.

I looked at that suspension bridge and my head began to spin. The waves below reached up like grasping fingers waiting to pull us into the wild water.

'It's all right,' said Grandad with a laugh. 'You can't fall off. The net would stop you.'

Fred's Bridge had two string walls made out of fishing net. The thought of stumbling against one of them made me feel sick. All right, you wouldn't fall. But how would you feel at that moment of terror as the net gave way under your weight? Just the idea of it made me feel like heaving up my breakfast.

And what if the ropes broke? Like they do in the movies. If that happened we would both be thrown to our deaths.

Grandad walked on to the swaying bridge. 'Come on,' he said.

I watched him cross. The bridge swayed with every step. I waited until he had crossed right over to the other side. Then I put one foot onto the wooden slats. And then the other.

Oh, I couldn't stand it. I couldn't do it. Not just walking across like that. I dropped down on my hands and knees and started to crawl. I made my way forward like a cowardly dog.

'Come on,' yelled Grandad. 'You can do it.'

Finally I reached the other side. Grandad smiled and rubbed my hair. 'Don't worry about it,' he said. 'We all have our own demons to face.'

'Where's Sandy?' I asked.

We both stared back across the bridge. Sandy was whimpering and putting one paw on the slats and then backing away. She was too frightened to cross. She didn't like the look of the bridge.

'Go home, girl,' Grandad yelled. Sandy just sat there. She was going to wait.

Grandad looked at his watch. 'We'd better get a move on,' he said. 'It's still a long way.'

3

It was too. We walked along the cliff tops for another hour before we stopped. Grandad was puffing. He sat down and rested against a gnarled tree. All of the leaves had been ripped off by the wind. The branches shook like fingers on a dancing skeleton. Nothing could stand up to that wind. It killed everything except the tough grass, which bent and rippled like the surface of the sea.

Clouds ripped across the sky. 'A storm's coming,' said Grandad. 'The wind is picking up. I think we'd better go back.'

I was really disappointed. We hadn't even started fishing and now he wanted to go back.

Suddenly Grandad cried out in pain. He clutched at his chest and screwed up his face in agony.

'Grandad,' I yelled. 'What's the matter? What's up?'

'My ticker,' he groaned. 'My ticker's playing up.'

I looked at his wrist. 'Your watch?' I shouted.

'My heart,' he said. His face grew white and he clutched his chest with his right hand.

He slumped against the tree with his eyes closed. 'Grandad,' I shrieked. 'Grandad.'

He didn't move. He didn't answer. He was gasping

for air with a terrible rasping sound. I looked around for help. But there was no one there.

There was nothing I could do but leave Grandad lying under the bare tree. I ran and ran and ran. My sides ached. A terrible pain stabbed into the left side of my stomach. I gasped and wheezed and fought for every breath.

And with each step the wind grew stronger. Soon it was ripping and tearing at my clothes. My hair was lashing my face. I felt like I was forcing my way through an invisible wall. The wind was my enemy. Pushing me back. Slowing me down. Trying to topple me off the cliff.

I hated that wind.

But I battled against it. Step after step. Leaping, struggling, pushing myself against the terrible storm.

Until at last I reached Fred's Bridge. It's funny how you can find courage when you need it. I ran straight onto the bridge without even thinking. It swayed and rocked wildly but I hardly noticed. I lurched crazily with every step but in no time I reached the other side where Sandy was still waiting patiently. She whimpered and jumped up at me.

'Come on, girl,' I shouted. 'Grandad's in trouble.'

I ran and ran and ran with Sandy at my heels.

Many times I stopped and held my side. The pain was sharp and piercing. The wind grew into a shrieking, howling monster. Trying everything it could to stop me.

But in the end I reached the house. I burst into the kitchen and shouted. The words all came out in a rush.

'Grandma,' I yelled. 'Grandad's ticker is playing up.'

4

The people from the State Emergency Service came quickly. They wouldn't let me go with them. They wouldn't let Grandma go either. We had to wait. For ages and ages. The storm whipped and raged and ranted. Night fell.

I wondered if the people from the SES would be able to get across the bridge to Grandad. What if it had been damaged by the wind?

They did get across the bridge to Grandad. But when they reached him his heart had stopped beating. He was dead. There was nothing they could do for him so they had to wait for the storm to end. They had to stay there on the cliff all night with Grandad. That's what the police told us.

Grandma and Sandy and I sat and waited as the hours ticked by. We hugged each other and let the tears mix on our cheeks. We stared out of the window and watched the storm die in the dawn's new day.

In the morning the SES carried Grandad back to our house on a stretcher covered in a blanket. An ambulance was waiting to take him away.

Grandma made me stay inside but she went out and looked under the blanket. I saw her lift Grandad's cold, stiff arm and peer at his wrist. Then she spoke to one of the men. He sadly shook his head.

When she came back I said, 'Was the watch there?'

She threw a glance at the kitchen clock and said, 'He must have dropped it. It will have stopped ticking by now. I won't be able to keep my promise.'

I gritted my teeth. 'I'll get it for you,' I said in a determined voice. 'I'll find it.'

Grandma shook her head. 'No,' she said. 'It's no use. I was supposed to keep it ticking. To never let it stop. To remind me that for all those years his heart had gone on beating next to mine. But now it's stopped and the promise is already broken.'

I didn't know what to say. I just kept thinking of

that watch lying there on the cliff top. Silent. Still. With frozen hands. Not ticking. The cruel wind covering it with dust.

I hated that wind.

5

There was a funeral.

And there was a wake where everyone came and brought cakes and casseroles. Friends called in and left cards and flowers. They told stories about Grandad and the old days. There was laughter and tears. Every day for a month people visited or phoned.

But in the end there was just me and Grandma. She had not smiled. Not once since Grandad had died.

She would slowly go about her daily jobs. And when they were done, she would sit on the porch with the wind gently blowing her hair and watch the sea.

But she never smiled. Not once.

'It's the watch,' I said. 'Isn't it?'

She nodded. 'I didn't keep it ticking. I let it stop. I broke my word.'

'You couldn't help it,' I said. 'They wouldn't let you go.'

I wanted to make her happy. I wanted to cheer her up. I wanted to see her smile again. I made her breakfast in bed. I told her stories and jokes. I brought her ropes and buoys and craypots that washed up on the shore. I gave her hugs and read aloud to her.

But nothing worked. Nothing would take the sadness out of her eyes. Or put the smile back on her lips.

Even Sandy's snuffling wet nose and excited barking couldn't cheer her up.

Then one day a terrible thought hit me. What if *Grandma's* ticker stopped? What if *her* heart stopped beating? What if she just gave up?

That's when I decided. That's when I made up my mind to find that watch. Even if it *had* stopped ticking.

6

I packed some water and food and started off along the cliff. I didn't tell Grandma. No one knew where I was going. Except Sandy. She trotted a few steps behind me. She didn't chase rabbits or birds. She stayed right with me. Almost as if she knew what was going on.

The wind grew stronger and stronger. Why did it always try to stop me? I lowered my head and pushed my way against it to the bridge.

Or what was left of it.

The wooden slats were still intact. But the netting sides had been ripped out by the wind. They flew like tattered flags from the ropes above. There was nothing to stop anyone falling straight down into the sea. The waves were moving mountains again today. The bridge shook and buckled like a road rearing in an earthquake.

I hid the sight from my eyes with my hands. I couldn't look. I couldn't cross. I couldn't move.

How long I crouched there is hard to say. But then I started to think of Grandma. How many ticks did her heart have left? Could it stop beating just because it was sad?

I crawled out onto the planks. There were no sides. There was nothing to stop me hurtling down into the clutches of the angry waves below. I closed my eyes and went forward on my hands and knees. But it was too terrifying. I collapsed onto my stomach and moved forward on my belly like a snake instead. I wriggled along the heaving surface, desperately grabbing one plank after another, and dragging my legs behind me. The bridge swayed and rocked with renewed fury in the howling wind.

Slowly, slowy, I inched forward. For one crazy second I thought about throwing myself down just to end the agony. But in the end I beat it. I made it to the other side with my eyes still closed.

Something wet touched my face. Wet and sloppy. It was Sandy. She had followed me across. How she didn't get blown off the bridge I'll never know.

We struggled on against the wind. Sometimes rain squalls would sweep in from the sea and lash my face. My nose and the tips of my ears were so cold that they hurt. But we kept going. I had to find that watch. Even if it had stopped ticking I felt that it might somehow help Grandma. And keep her going.

I crossed a huge sand dune. The wind picked up the grains of sand and hurled them into my face, like a volley of tiny arrows.

I hated the wind.

7

At last I reached the place where Grandad had died. The lonely tree still clawed at the sky with its bare limbs.

I began to search among the grass and rocks. Grandad had been wearing the watch when I had left him. And the SES had brought him back on a stretcher. So it must be around somewhere. I began to circle the tree, inspecting every inch of ground. I walked slowly, gradually working my way further and further out.

Nothing. No sign of it.

Sandy was snuffling and sniffing herself. Was she looking for rabbits? Or did she understand? Did she want to find the watch too?

After about an hour I stopped and slumped down against the tree just like Grandad had when he'd died. The watch was nowhere to be seen. It was useless. Grandad had died leaning against that tree. He hadn't moved. But the watch wasn't there.

A terrible feeling of emptiness seemed to drain away my strength. I leaned back and closed my eyes. The cold wind buffeted my face.

'Ruff, ruff, ruff.' Sandy began to bark like crazy.

I jumped up to see what she was barking about. 'Good girl,' I shouted. 'You little beauty.'

8

I don't remember much about the journey back. I was so happy.

Once again I had to face the swaying bridge with its broken net. But I wasn't terrified like the first time. I just wanted to get home. I wanted to give Grandma the news.

In my rush across the bridge I slipped and fell sprawling on my face. For a moment I was nearly sick again. But I jumped up and almost ran to the other side. We pelted back along the cliffs to the house.

I burst into the kitchen. 'Grandma,' I shouted. 'I've found Grandad's watch.'

No smile. She didn't even look at it. 'You shouldn't have gone,' she said. 'It was too dangerous. And anyway, his watch stopped ticking long ago.'

'No,' I yelled. 'It didn't. It's still going.'

'Because you put it on your wrist,' said Grandma. 'That has wound it up. It's not the same. It stopped ticking.'

'It didn't,' I shouted. 'Look, it's showing the right time.'

Grandma took the watch from my outstretched hand. 'You didn't reset it?'

'No.'

'But it's been over a month. How could it have kept ticking all that time?'

She smiled when I told her. The biggest smile ever. And I knew her heart would go on ticking for a long time to come.

'Grandad strapped it onto a branch of the tree,' I said. 'The wind kept it moving.'

Outside the clouds scudded across the sky. A sudden strong gust hit the house and made it tremble.

'I *love* the wind,' I said.

Guts

'It likes to eat people,' said Mr Borg. 'It will eat dogs, cats, snakes and even cows. But its favourite food is human beings.'

'It eats people?' I yelped.

'People,' said Mr Borg. 'Loves 'em. It's a real guts.'

My mouth was hanging open. But my sister Danni's teeth were firmly clenched.

'What sort of people?' I asked.

'Its favourite is kids,' said Mr Borg. 'Especially cheeky brats like you two.'

'Get real,' said Danni.

'Oh, yeah,' said Mr Borg in a mean voice. 'Well, go and take a look for yourself. Go and pay a visit to the Lost Mine. In fact do us all a favour and get lost yourselves.'

Mr Borg gave a hearty laugh. He thought this was very funny.

'Ghosts don't eat,' said Danni. 'They can't even pick things up.'

'The Spirit of the Forest is not your normal ghost,' said Mr Borg. 'It doesn't eat with its hands. Or its mouth. But it devours things. Oh, yes. A horrible sound. You should hear it crunch.'

'You're just trying to scare us,' I said. 'So that Dad will leave and sell our land to you. Well, you're not getting it. Ever.'

Mr Borg's dog, Hacker, started to bark and growl and snap at us through the back window of his Jaguar.

Mr Borg scowled. 'We'll see about that,' he said. He flattened the accelerator and drove off in a cloud of dust.

Danni and I walked slowly back to our little farm by the river.

Things were not going too good. Dad made a living by putting up fences for the big land owners. But times were tough in the bush and he wasn't getting much work. We were nearly broke. If things didn't improve the bank was going to sell us up.

'I couldn't stand it if we had to move into a town,' I said to Danni.

She looked around at the little farm that had been

our home since the day we were born. 'Mr Borg is not getting this land. This is ours.'

We stared defiantly around our little farm. We had the best spot on the whole river. All around us were the high mountains of the national park. The peaks were covered in tropical rainforest. It was the most beautiful place in the world. I couldn't even bear to think about leaving it.

Mr Borg wanted to build a casino resort. He was a developer of the worst sort.

2

As soon as we stepped into the kitchen I could tell that something was wrong. Dad was walking around the room kicking at things and muttering angrily under his breath.

'What's up?' I said.

He didn't answer for a second or two. He couldn't bring himself to say the words. Finally he spat it out. 'The Land Rover's gone.'

'Where?' shouted Danni.

'Someone nicked it. Last night. I left it down in the bottom paddock. Now all that's left are a few tracks in the mud.'

Danni and I gasped. Without the Land Rover, Dad wouldn't be able to get any work.

'We're finished if we don't get it back,' he said bitterly. 'It wasn't even insured.'

'Who would want the Land Rover?' I said.

'Come on,' said Danni. 'Use your brains.'

'Mr Borg,' I gasped. 'To force us to sell up.'

'Dad,' I yelled. 'Let's go. Let's get him. Let's flatten him. Let's beat the sh–'

Dad shook his head. 'Getting into a fight won't achieve anything. And we don't know that it was Borg who nicked it. And we couldn't prove it anyway. He's not likely to have left it in his backyard.'

'Where then?' said Danni.

'In the river,' said Dad. 'Or at the bottom of a cliff. Maybe down a mine shaft.'

When Dad said that my mind started to tick over.

'I'll have to go to the police,' said Dad. 'Not that it will do any good. We'll never see that car again, that's for sure.'

Dad went off to report the theft to the police. He was going to go to the bank as well. To see if they would extend his bank loan.

Danni and I walked down to the back paddock and examined the tyre tracks. They didn't tell us much. We followed them along the river and out of the bottom gate. They disappeared down the road.

'If Borg took the car,' said Danni. 'Where would he have dumped it?'

I went over Dad's words in my mind. 'In the river. Or at the bottom of a cliff. Maybe down –'

'A mine shaft,' I shouted.

'The Lost Mine,' said Danni. 'That's why he was telling us all the bulldust about the Spirit of the Forest. A ghost that eats people.'

'That was a story to stop us going there,' I said. 'To scare us off.'

We were so excited. We couldn't wait for Dad to get back so that we could all go up to the Lost Mine and look for the Land Rover.

So we waited. And we waited. And we waited.

Finally, just at the sun was setting, we saw Dad walking home.

Walking.

Of course. He had to walk. Our four-wheel drive was gone. No wonder he was late.

Dad sort of swaggered into the gate, his head held high. But he couldn't fool us. We could tell he was trying to act cheerful so that we wouldn't get upset.

He didn't want to talk about it but we finally dragged the truth out of him.

'The bank won't extend our loan,' he said. 'We can't buy a new Land Rover. We can't even hang on to the property. The bank is going to sell us up. But don't worry, kids. Life in the city isn't that bad.'

'Borg will buy our property,' I said.

Dad nodded.

'We know where the Land Rover is,' said Danni.

Dad listened to her story carefully. He let her finish but he kept shaking his head all the way through.

'No,' he said. 'We're not going up to the Lost Mine. It's too dangerous. No one is allowed up there because of the hidden mine shafts. Lots of people have gone there and never been seen again.'

'The Spirit of . . .' said Danni.

'There *is* something odd about that forest,' said Dad. 'But there's no spirit. Borg told you that story so that we *would* go there. If the car is there it means he wants us to find it.'

'Why?' I said.

'So that he can gloat. It will be smashed or down a mine shaft. We will know that he did it but we won't be able to prove a thing.'

'I thought you loved that car,' said Danni.

'Of course I love it,' said Dad. 'That's why I can't bear to find it all smashed and wrecked.' He forced a grin. 'Look, don't be so gloomy, you two. I'll go into town tomorrow. And arrange for the bank to get on with the sale. You never know. We might even get a really good price.'

Danni and I went out onto the porch and sat listening to the crickets chirping in the warm summer air.

'Do you know where I'm going tomorrow?' I said.

Danni gave a grin. 'The same place as me,' she said.

3

Danni and I stared along the narrow track that disappeared into the forest.

'Look,' said Danni. 'Someone's been here. Maybe a fire truck.' She pointed at a set of wheel tracks in the mud.

'Maybe our Land Rover,' I said. I could hardly stop my voice from shaking with excitement.

I hitched up my pack and took the first step into forbidden territory.

'Do you believe that story about the Spirit of the Forest?' I asked Danni.

She shrugged. 'They reckon that this forest is magical. Anyone who hurts the trees or digs holes suffers a terrible fate. All the workers from the Lost Mine just disappeared. Never seen again. No one ever comes up here.'

I didn't say anything. I just hoped the story wasn't true.

We trudged on and on and on. The track wound through deep gullies and over creek beds. Always heading up. Gradually the forest grew denser. The air was hot and clammy.

'We should have left a note,' I said. 'What if we get lost?'

'If we stick to the track we can't get lost,' said Danni.

I gave a shiver. 'We have to turn back by lunchtime,' I said. 'Otherwise we won't get back by dark.' The thought of spending the night on the mountain was making me nervous.

We kept on. With aching legs and blistered feet we forced our way up the mountain. Sometimes we would break out of the forest and find ourselves staring down into the valley. The tiny houses told us quite clearly how far away we were from people. And help.

After another three hours of struggling uphill, the track levelled out and headed into a dark damp gully lined with ferns and moss.

I slumped down onto a log. 'Twelve o'clock,' I said. 'Time to turn back. We need to get home before Dad.'

'Give it one hour,' said Danni. 'One more hour.'

So we did.

And exactly fifty-nine minutes later we saw what we had come for.

'Look,' I screamed.

4

The Land Rover stood in the middle of a quickly flowing stream. The bonnet was up but there was no one around.

On the other side of the water we could see an abandoned mine site. The shaft itself was just a black hole in the side of a cliff. Nearby were a number of sagging sheds with dusty broken windows. The whole area was littered with rusting machinery that had grass and shrubs growing out of it. A huge pile of grey rocks spewed down the cliff face. All sorts of rubbish cluttered the site. Old oil drums, a kettle, a meat safe, a broken oil lamp, several rotting mattresses – the last remaining signs of long-dead miners.

We waded into the stream and I stared at the engine of the Land Rover. 'Water on the distributor,' I said.

'Easily fixed,' said Danni.

We were both so excited. Dad loved this car. We all did. It wouldn't take a second to dry the distributor and start the engine. Danni looked inside.

'Uh-oh,' she said.

'What?' I asked.

'No key. The ignition key has gone.'

Drat. I could dry off the wet ignition leads. And I could drive the Land Rover. No worries. But how to start it up without a key? That was another matter altogether. We had to get going quickly. Before Borg came and found us. Before . . .

'What's that?' said Danni suddenly.

We both stood still with the water swirling around our knees and listened.

'A dog,' I said. 'Somewhere far off.'

'Down the mine,' said Danni. 'Let's go.'

'Let's go?' I said. 'Don't be crazy. Anyone could be down there. *Anything* could be down there.'

'That's Hacker,' said Danni. 'Borg's dog. I'd know that growl anywhere. Find the dog and we find Borg. Find Borg and we find the key to the Land Rover.'

My sister had plenty of guts. I was scared but I couldn't let her go alone. We waded across the stream and walked carefully between the tumble-down sheds.

Everything was as silent as a grave. The buildings were overgrown with blackberries and weeds. Totally deserted. A door creaked eerily on its rusty hinges. Almost as if a hidden hand had given it a push.

'Ghosts,' I said.

'Rubbish,' said Danni.

I grabbed her arm. 'I'm not going into the mine until we've thought this through,' I said.

We sat down on a log in silence. After a bit I noticed something moving. A revolting little cane toad. It was creeping through the grass towards a dirty glass jar. Inside the jar was a small piece of steak.

Steak? Where had that come from?

The toad suddenly hopped into the jar. But before it could grab the meat something really weird happened. The toad gave a terrible shudder and froze. Just stopped dead. Then it began to fade. I could see right through its body. It was only a faint outline, almost as if it was made of mist. Or smoke. Then it vanished.

The jar wobbled and made a noise. It sounded like . . . well, yes, like a tiny burp. Then it vanished too. Into thin air.

'Aaagh,' I screamed.

'What?'

'A toad just vanished. And a jar.'

Danni gave me a little pat on the head. 'If you could make cane toads vanish,' she said. 'You would be the most popular person in Australia. Come on. Let's go.'

5

We shouldered our packs and walked into the mouth of the black mine. A terrible smell filled the air. A foul, retch-making stench.

'Uurgh,' said Danni. 'A dead possum.'

I stared at the rotting corpse and held a tissue over my mouth. The possum's nose had fallen off and its fur was rotting.

Sitting right on top of it was another cane toad. Having a feast. Feeding on the carcass.

'Yuck,' I said with a shudder.

Danni took out her torch and stepped carefully into the darkness of the mine. 'Let's get going,' she said.

The tunnel grew blacker. Water dripped onto the wet earth beneath our feet. We followed twisted railway tracks deeper and deeper into the mountainside. Suddenly Danni stopped. She was shining her torch on something. A wooden packing case. Inside was a small dead fish.

Danni reached down, 'Well, look at that,' she said.

'Don't touch it,' I yelled.

Something dark flitted past our heads and grabbed the fish. At first I couldn't work out what it was. The fish seemed to be covered by a ball of quivering fur.

'A feral cat,' I gasped.

The cat did not get a chance to eat. There was no mistaking it. Unbelievable as it may seem, in the torchlight we saw what we saw. For a second the feral cat waved its tail. Then it grew still. And pale. Its skin turned clear and for a moment it resembled a small ice sculpture. Then *whoosh* it vanished into

steam. The box trembled and began to fade. It gave
a little 'hic' and vanished.

Danni's eyes grew round.

'The fish was bait,' I whispered. 'And the box was
a –'

'Ghost box,' said Danni.

'The Spirit of the Forest,' I said. 'It doesn't like
mines. Or miners. Or anything that comes here.' We
both backed away, pushing ourselves against the
wall. It was cold that far underground. But my hands
were sweating. I tried to swallow but fear seemed to
paralyse my muscles.

I thought about what we had seen. 'The ghost can
make itself into any shape,' I said. I reminded Danni
about the first cane toad and she shook her head in
horror.

'It could turn itself into a jar,' I said in a hoarse
voice.

'Or a box,' Danni whispered.

'Any hollow object. It can make itself into that
shape,' I said slowly. 'And any living thing that
wanders into it is eaten.'

'Turned to vapour,' said Danni.

'No, turned into a spectre,' I said. 'Dead, gone,
vanished from this world. Into the next.'

We stared at each other in the light of the torch. Then without a word we both started to run. Scrambling, screaming back towards the entrance. We fled into the blackness, not knowing what cold hand might reach down and grab us. The beam from our torch bounced crazily from the mine's wall.

6

Finally we stopped. Sucking in the cold air with noisy gulps. Trying to see into the gloom.

Danni was peering at something. 'What's that?' she gasped. 'It wasn't there before.'

We stared at a huge steel bank vault. The door hung open. Inside it was empty. Except for something small, made of metal. It glinted in the torchlight.

'A key,' gasped Danni.

'The Land Rover key,' I said. 'Fabulous.' I stumbled forward but this time Danni grabbed me.

'Don't,' she said. 'It's bait. And look. It's not even a real key. You can see through it. It's a ghost key.'

Suddenly a terrible snarling howl filled the air. We turned. And there he was. Not a spectre but our deadly enemy. Borg. And his dog, Hacker.

105

The huge animal bared its long teeth and dripped saliva.

Borg's face was filled with hatred. 'Where's your father?' he shouted angrily.

'Outside,' I lied. 'He'll be here any minute.'

'Good,' said Borg. 'He's the one I want. But you two will do for starters.'

Now I realised what this was all about. Borg knew about the Spirit of the Forest. He wanted Dad to disappear so that he could get our farm. He had lured us up here on purpose.

Borg spoke in a low voice to his dog. 'Back 'em up, boy, back 'em up.'

Hacker lowered his head and growled horribly. Danni and I started to back away towards the vault. The dog was herding us like sheep. Straight into the gaping vault.

'You want the key,' said Borg. 'Go get it.'

Hacker suddenly lunged forward with open jaws. Straight through my legs. Straight into the vault.

Why had he gone past us? Why? Why? Suddenly I realised. The key had been removed because no one took the bait. And in its place was an enormous bone.

The dog grabbed the bone and then gave a terrible

howl. His fur stood up on end and began to move like ghostly grass in a breeze. In a flash the dog was nothing but a pale image. Then he vanished.

The vault shimmered for a second. Then it burped loudly and was gone.

Danni and I stood so still that our feet might have been nailed to the ground. The ghost-vault had swallowed the dog. It was a nasty, savage dog. But still and all – it was a dog, a living being. It had perished in front of our eyes.

Borg shook his head. His eyes grew round. Not with sorrow. But with selfish fear.

Without warning he snatched the torch from Danni's hand and ran down the tunnel.

'Come back, come back,' I yelled. 'Give us our torch back.'

The tunnel echoed with his reply. A piercing, hollow laugh. In a flash he rounded a corner and disappeared from sight. We were alone in the pitch dark. Without light.

'I'm scared,' I said.

'So am I,' said Danni. 'But we have to get out of here.'

I silently reached out and felt for her hand. We began to make our way back along the terrible tunnel with our fingers locked together. We bumped into the walls many times. We slipped and slid. But neither of us put into words the fears that gripped our guts. What if somewhere in the darkness lay a ghostly box or cage? Waiting for us to fall inside.

Would we end up disappearing in a burp or a hiccup? Zapped. Vaporised. Swallowed.

7

I don't know how long we stumbled along but finally we came upon a split in the tunnel. We both felt about in the darkness with our hands. There were two passages.

'Which way?' I said. 'Which is the way out? I can't see a thing.'

'I bet these tunnels wander around for miles,' said Danni. 'Some of them might end in the wells and deep holes. If we take the wrong turn we might fall down a shaft and never get out.'

I gave a shiver and gasped at the thought.

'Take a breath,' I said.

'What?'

'Take a deep breath. Through your nose.'

I heard Danni breathe deeply. But I didn't see her smile because it was so dark.

'This way,' she yelled. 'You're a genius, Nelson.'

We hurried on, following the stink of the dead possum.

My mind was filled with crazy thoughts. Was the spirit waiting for us somewhere in the darkness ahead? Had Borg escaped and taken the Land Rover? Was he pushing it into some deep shaft at this very moment? And Dad. Poor Dad. Without his car. Without his children. How would he manage? How would he find the strength to go on?

'Light,' screamed Danni. 'I see light.'

We staggered to the entrance of the tunnel. Or where the entrance had been. The way was blocked by a door. A door with a brightly lit window. I peered through and saw the most amazing sight.

A small cottage had been built up against the opening of the mine. Inside was an old bush table with rough wooden chairs. A fire burnt in a wood stove. And on the table a roast chicken sat steaming on a plate.

I looked around. Was this a different entrance? No. Because over there against the wall I could see the stinking carcass of the dead possum. Someone had built the cottage right across the way out.

Danni peered in at the roast chicken and licked her lips.

But she wasn't fooled. And neither was I. 'Bait,' was all she said.

We both knew that whoever stepped into that cottage was going to meet a terrible fate. But we had to get out. We had to reach the sunshine. And get to the Land Rover.

I looked around. Then I ran over to the dead possum. I held one hand over my mouth. And with the other I picked up the rubbery nose from where it lay on the ground.

I rushed over to the door, opened it and threw in the nose. 'There,' I yelled. 'You want food. Try that.' I quickly slammed the door shut.

Everything was still. Then the door flew open and the nose shot out and bounced off the mine wall like a bullet. There was a large gurgling noise like someone being sick.

'It only likes live meat,' said Danny.

I scanned the walls of the mine. I needed something alive. But there was nothing. Except Danni. And . . . there, sitting on a ledge. The revolting cane toad. I pulled my hand into my sleeve and grabbed the creepy creature. Then I opened the door of the cottage and threw the toad into the kitchen.

For a second the toad squirmed and then it grew still. And pale. Its skin turned clear and for a moment it was like a sliver of ice. Then *whoosh*, it vanished into steam. The whole cottage trembled and began to fade. It gave an enormous burp of satisfaction. The whole mine shook with the noise. It echoed down the tunnel like a belch in the guts of a giant.

We were safe.

That's what I thought for about two seconds. Until powerful hands grabbed my shoulders and threw me onto the ground. The air was knocked from my lungs and I lay there gasping for breath.

'Thanks,' yelled Borg. 'Good thinking. I couldn't have done it without you.'

He rushed past me out of the tunnel. Danni bent down beside me with a worried look. 'Are you okay, Nelson?' she asked.

I couldn't answer for several minutes. I just couldn't breathe. Finally I managed a couple of words. 'The car,' I gasped.

Danni helped me out into the fresh air and we made our way towards the river. I had to rest on Danni's shoulder. We moved slowly.

Finally we reached the stream. The Land Rover had gone.

'Borg,' said Danni.

There was nothing more to say. Borg had beaten us to the car. We would never see it again. In my heart I knew that we were only kids and we couldn't defeat a grown man. Not on our own. Borg would destroy the car. And no one would believe us.

We had gone through all this horror for nothing.

We walked sadly back towards the road. Trying to work out why the spirit ate some things and not others.

'The spirit hates anything that harms the forest,' I said. 'Anything foreign. Anything introduced.'

'Cane toads,' panted Danni.

'Dogs,' I said. 'And feral cats.'

'And ...' said Danni. 'People who want to dig or chop things down.'

We both looked back and then hurried out of the forest as fast as we could go.

8

Dad was waiting for us when we reached home. He was out the front washing the Land Rover in the last light of the day. 'Look,' he yelled. 'It was in Borg's backyard after all. The police found it last night.'

'Last night?' I said.

'Yes,' said Dad. 'Around midnight. I've spent all day cleaning it up.'

'All day,' I said. 'But . . .' I didn't finish the sentence. Danni was shaking her head at me. No one would ever believe our story.

And that is the end of the story. Borg was never seen again.

'What do you think happened to him?' Danni asked me later that night.

I gave a laugh. 'Well,' I said. 'Let's just say that he should have thrown a cane toad into that Land Rover before he climbed into it.'

Shadows

Think of the meanest thing you ever did.

Okay. So why did you do it?

You don't know, do you? No one knows why they suddenly do something mean.

Even your mum and your dad can be awful now and then. Or your lovely old grandma. Or the prime minister. Even the bishop in his church. Everyone is sneaky sometimes. Greedy sometimes. Rude sometimes. Selfish sometimes. No one is perfect. It is okay to be human.

Sometimes, when I am bad-tempered, my mum will say, 'Richard is not himself today.'

And this makes me wonder. If you are not yourself, who are you?

1

On the day I found out, I was walking around the fairground without a worry in the world. I had no money but there was plenty to look at for nothing. The animal nursery. The man on stilts. The busker playing the violin. The man throwing fire-sticks into the air. All the stalls selling jewellery and scented candles. Little kids with their balloons. Mothers and fathers pushing prams.

Yes. The best things in life are free.

Except for show bags, the Ghost Train, the Sledgehammer, the Rocket to Mars, the Rotor, the Hall of Mirrors, and Bubbles Bo Bo.

All of them cost five dollars each to get in. And I had no dollars. And no cents. I was broke.

Actually, the Hall of Mirrors gave me the creeps. There was a little man sitting outside selling tickets. His name was Mr Image. He wore an old baseball hat and had a five o'clock shadow. And he had mean eyes. They seemed to see right into you. He made me shiver. But all the same, I wanted to go in. I wanted to have a look at myself in the Hall of Mirrors.

But not as much as I wanted to have a look at

Bubbles Bo Bo. She was a beautiful lady sitting in a bath full of bubbles with nothing on.

Not a stitch on. That's what all the kids at school reckoned anyway.

I walked past her tent and pretended not to be gazing up at the painting outside. The one of Bubbles sitting in the bath with a bare leg held up in the air.

You couldn't see all the other bits. Bubbles was covered in bubbles, if you know what I mean.

Suddenly I had an idea. A way to get to see Bubbles Bo Bo for nothing.

I slowly walked up to the guy who was selling tickets. He was a rough-looking bloke with a whole heap of earrings and tattoos.

'Excuse me,' I said. 'But would you like someone to sweep up inside? For nothing.'

He looked down at me with a big grin. That grew bigger. And bigger. He threw back his head and started to laugh. He had long yellow teeth and he laughed so madly that I could see right inside his mouth. The dangling thing up the back was wobbling around like crazy. 'Hey, Harry,' he yelled. 'Get a load of this kid. He's trying to sneak a look at Bubbles by offering to sweep the floor.'

My face started to burn. I didn't know where to hide. Everyone in the world seemed to be grinning and looking at me.

A toothless, skinny man hurried out and started to cackle like a chook. He doubled up, clutching his side and gasping, 'Wants to sweep the floor – for nothing. Wants a free peek at Bubbles. Ha, ha ho, ho ha.'

Oh, if only I could have vanished. If only I could have gone up in smoke. All the passers-by seemed to be watching me. Knowing what was inside my head. What a sleaze. That's what they were all thinking.

I started to stumble away. Trying to find somewhere to hide. Looking for a rock to crawl under.

Suddenly I heard a voice.

'You can sweep *my* floor. And I'll pay you for it.'

It was Mr Image. The man of mirrors.

'Come back in the morning,' he said. 'At first light. I'll pay you ten dollars to sweep the Hall of Mirrors.'

A cold weight seemed to be sliding down my throat. Like an iceblock inside me it travelled down, down, down, until even my toes started to shiver.

He smiled. A cold smile. As if no one was home behind those mean eyes.

Everything inside me told me to run away. But I thought about the money. And Bubbles Bo Bo. And nodded my head.

2

The next morning I arrived at the fairground just as the sun was rising. All the show people were getting ready for the day. An old man was washing down his elephant. Two guys in a truck were unloading packets of hot dogs. A kid about my age was taking the covers off the dodgem cars.

I walked nervously over to the Hall of Mirrors. 'Ah, Richard,' said Mr Image. 'You've come to work.'

He handed me a bucket of water and a mop, and disappeared into the large gloomy tent. I followed him.

'How did you know my –' I started to say.

Mr Image interrupted me in a voice like a wet whisper. 'Use the mop,' he said. 'A broom raises dust and it gets on the mirrors.'

He poured some liquid soap into the bucket and walked away. His feet made a rustling sound as if he was walking on dry leaves.

The tent was filled with corridors that were lined

with mirrors. Like a maze with openings shooting off here and there. It was gloomy, which was strange for a place filled with reflections.

I started to clean up underneath a bent mirror. A fat, fat Richard copied my every move. I walked backwards and forwards, watching my image grow bigger and smaller.

All of the mirrors gave weird reflections. Fat. Thin. Ugly. Bent. Upside down. Crinkled.

I mopped and stared. Mopped and stared. It was lonely. It was quiet. It was creepy. Inside the Hall of Mirrors.

The silent morning moved on. I seemed a million miles away from the show and all its life outside. I was alone but surrounded by dozens of people. Bent and horrible copies of myself mopping the floors all around me. Repulsive reflections holding their warped mops in twisted fingers.

I shivered. Why had I taken this terrible job? I wanted to burst out of this tent and flee into the real world outside. But somewhere down there. In the gloom. Was Mr Image. Moving around like a rat in a cupboard. I was too scared to run out on him. He was the sort of person who would follow you. Not let go.

Minutes ticked by. Or was it hours? It was hard to tell. My ugly companions mopped silently alongside me. They rested silently. Copied my every move without a sound.

I started to mop more quickly. I wanted to get it over with. Finish up. Take my money and run. Faster and faster I mopped. And faster and faster the freaky copies moved with me.

I turned a corner and faced a door.

On it was a sign which simply said: RICHARD'S ROOM.

3

A small building stood within the tent. Made of steel. About twice the size of a toilet.

Richard's Room? What did that mean? Had Mr Image put that sign there especially for me? Or was there another Richard? And what was inside?

I didn't know whether I was supposed to sweep in there or not. 'Hey,' I called out. 'Hey.' The silent army of terrible copies in the mirrors mouthed my words in silence. Jagged, torn mouths of every shape seemed to be laughing at me. Copies of myself.

It was like being left alone in bed in the dark

of night. You hear a noise. You want to call out 'Mum'. But if there is a burglar, if there is an intruder, he will know where you are. And come for you like a shadow.

'Don't be silly,' I said to myself. 'Don't be stupid. It's just a room.'

I pushed open the door and stepped inside with my mop and bucket.

There was nothing in the room except one mirror, which filled up a whole wall. Not a trick mirror. It was straight and flat like the ones in your bathroom at home. The wall opposite the mirror was covered by a picture. A huge painting which reached from the floor to the ceiling. A scene with a flat plain that was edged with jungle growth.

The door clicked shut behind me. Just a soft sound. But I knew, I just knew that it was as final as the clang of a noisy lock on a jail cell.

There was no handle.

Just a keyhole.

No way of escape.

'Hey,' I screamed. 'Help. Let me out.' My words were soaked up by the thick walls. I knew that no one could hear me. I kicked and shouted and punched the door. It didn't move. Not even a rattle.

I was alone.

Or was I? The mirror glowed faintly as if it had a light of its own. I moved over and stared into it. The warmth from my body drained out through my feet and I shivered in horror. It was *not* an ordinary mirror. I could see the reflection of the wall behind me. The flat plain. The jungle. The vines and creepers and thorns. The towering trees. They were all there.

But I wasn't.

I couldn't see my own reflection. It was just as if I wasn't there.

I turned back to the door and began kicking and screaming and yelling. I kicked until my foot hurt. But no one came. I was locked away from the world in this silent room. I might as well have been in a coffin way under the ground. No one could hear me. No one except Mr Image knew where I was.

I stared into the softly glowing mirror. Something had changed. Something was different. There, across the plain. In a tree. On the edge of the jungle was something like a coconut on a tree. But it was moving. It ducked back out of sight.

A face. Someone or something was living inside the mirror.

I turned back to the door. 'Get me out of here,' I screamed.

No reply. I turned back to the mirror. The figure was no longer in the tree. It was moving closer. Dodging from one clump of grass to the other. It saw me and stopped. Almost as if frozen by my gaze.

Could this really be happening? I rubbed my eyes and then stared. *Zip.* It had moved closer.

Now I could see the figure more clearly. It was a person. Staring at me from the cover of a small bush. A person who I thought I knew.

My heart was pounding like a million mallets. My hands were clammy and cold.

I tried to stop panic taking control of me. I tried to force my brain to think. I didn't want this mirror man to come closer. I had to help myself. There was no one else.

I snatched a glance at the door. How could I get out?

Then I turned back to the mirror. He had snuck up. And he wasn't a mirror man. He was a mirror boy. Sneaking forward every time I looked away. There was something about him. What was it?

I stared and stared, trying not to blink. He stared

back from a distance. Waiting for his chance to move forward.

Time passed. The seconds and minutes dragged by like a slug in the sunshine.

Who was he? I decided to find out. I closed my eyes and counted to five.

Oh, no. No, no, no. Now he was much, much closer. And I could see his face. I knew who he was.

Me. The boy was me. My nose, my ears, my hair. It was me but not me. Not a reflection. More like a living shadow.

He froze under my gaze. I was scared. More frightened than I have ever been in my life.

Think. Use your brain, Richard. That's what I told myself. He wouldn't or couldn't move forward while I was watching him.

I stared harder and harder. Not even blinking. He didn't like it. He didn't like me looking at him. Like a startled rabbit in the beam of a spotlight he blinked and shuffled. And started to move backwards.

'Go,' I said to my self in the mirror. 'Go, go, go.'

Slowly and then faster and faster, he moved away. Suddenly he turned and ran back into the jungle. He clambered up a tree. I could see him there.

A tiny distant face. Like a coconut in among the branches.

But I knew he was waiting. Looking for his chance to creep up.

'Ah, Richard,' said a soft, wet voice. 'There you are.'

4

I hadn't heard the door open. But I heard it click shut. And I knew who it was. Mr Image.

'Look at me,' he said.

I snatched a glance. He was staring into the mirror himself.

I knew his game. He wanted me to look away from the mirror. So that my mirror shadow could sneak up again.

I wasn't falling for that. No way.

'Look at me when I speak to you,' he hissed.

I was his prey. Like a fly in a spider's web.

But I was in control. There was no way I was going to take my eyes off that shadow-boy in the mirror. No way. It wasn't going to sneak up on me.

I edged away from Mr Image. If he grabbed me and wrestled me to the floor it would give my shadow time to run up. Mr Image moved with me. I could feel his jacket brushing against me.

'Look at me,' he screeched. He didn't grab me. He was transfixed. Staring into the mirror himself. Suddenly I realised why. There was another figure on the edge of the forest. Wearing a baseball cap. Unshaven and rough.

Mr Image had a shadow in the mirror himself.

Suddenly Mr Image lost his cool. He turned and grabbed me by the arm. 'Look here, look here,' he shouted.

But I didn't. I watched Mr Image's shadow sprint across the plain. Closer, closer. Jumping tussocks of grass. Dashing furiously towards us. The shadow was a copy of Mr Image. Another person like himself. Similar but not the same.

Mr Image grabbed my head. He twisted it towards himself. The pain in my neck was terrible. He was too strong for me. His own hatred and terror filled him with enormous strength.

I tried to speak but could only wheeze out the words, 'He's coming for you, Mr Image.'

He gave a strangled scream and let go. He peered into the mirror and saw his own shadow almost upon us. He stared and stared with wide-open eyes.

The shadow halted. Frozen by his gaze.

Mr Image was terrified of the other version of himself. But I wasn't. The copy of Mr Image was not a copy. It was an opposite. It had a kind, loving face with warm eyes.

My own hateful shadow was now halfway across the plain. It had snuck up when Mr Image grabbed my head. It had been waiting for its chance.

There in the mirror our shadows were held frozen by our stares. Neither of us could look away.

Mr Image began to walk backwards in the small room. The door behind was locked. But he could get out. He would know how to open the door. He was feeling in his pocket for the key.

'I think you need a little more time on your own,' he said.

He was going to leave me in there by myself. In the end I would have to take my eyes off the mirror. In the end I would have to fall asleep.

And then. And then.

The shadow would come for me.

I had to do something. I had to stop Mr Image rushing out of that door. He took another step backwards.

Suddenly I tore my eyes away from the mirror.

So did Mr Image. He was fumbling around with a key, trying to get it into the lock.

Out of the corner of my eye I saw the two shadows sprinting towards us. Mr Image's shadow was much closer. Almost up to us. My own was further back across the plain but running fast.

I looked around for a weapon. And found one.

'Cop this,' I shouted.

I threw the contents of the bucket into Mr Image's face. He screamed as the soapy water stung his eyes. He rubbed and wiped and wept in anger. But he couldn't see.

I fixed my shadow with a stare. And held him there. Inside his glass prison.

Mr Image's shadow was closing the gap. Running furiously. Bigger and closer. He was upon us. He leapt at the mirror from the other side. Like a horse clearing a hurdle he passed through the mirror. He landed at the feet of Mr Image, who was still screaming and rubbing his eyes.

Without a word the shadow grabbed Mr Image, lifted him above his head and twirled him around. Then he threw him into the mirror.

Mr Image screamed. A drawn-out, horrible cry. It was pitched so high that it hurt my ears. Then, like a glass broken by the voice of an opera singer, the mirror shattered. It fell to the floor in a million pieces. Mr Image was gone. Trapped inside his own mirror.

I turned and faced Mr Image's shadow.

He smiled at me with a warm, kind face. Little crinkles ran out beside his friendly eyes. The shadow was nothing to fear.

'Thanks,' he said. 'It's nice to be back.'

The shadow unlocked the door and took me out into the sunshine. 'Here's your pay,' he said. 'Ten dollars as agreed.'

He was such a nice man. He really was.

I smiled back at him. 'What was all that about?' I asked as I took the money. 'Did it really happen?'

He nodded. 'Everyone has a shadow,' he said. 'We all have a mixture. Strong and weak. Kind and cruel. Generous and mean.'

I shivered. 'I'm scared of my own shadow,' I said.

He nodded. 'Don't be,' he said. 'Take a walk in the sun. Think about it.'

5

I did take a walk. Past the animal nursery. The man on stilts. The busker playing the violin. The man throwing fire-sticks into the air, and all the stalls selling jewellery and scented candles. Little kids with their balloons. Mothers and fathers pushing prams.

It was really busy. But I didn't feel part of it. I couldn't stop thinking about my shadow.

The thing about it was this. Your shadow couldn't get you if you kept an eye on it. You could learn to live with the other side of yourself. It really wasn't so bad. We all do selfish things now and then. But so what? Just don't let it get out of hand.

That's how I figured it anyway. I wandered back towards the Hall of Mirrors. I wanted to ask the man from the mirror if I was right.

But he was gone. The grass was all flattened where the tent had been. He had packed up and left.

The guy with the earrings and the tattoos was still there with his tent though. I walked over to him. 'I've got a question,' I said.

He leered at me with a raised eyebrow. But he gave me the answer all the same.

'Five dollars,' he told me.

I pushed the five dollars into his hand and went in to have a peek at Bubbles Bo Bo.

Okay, so my mum wouldn't like it. And some people might even think I was a sleaze. But what the heck. There's two sides to all of us.

No one's perfect.

Squawk Talk

Go for it. That's what you've got to do. Look after number one. No one else will, that's for sure. Everyone thinks of themself first. Like that fool sitting opposite. He's only about my age. Look at him. Thinks he's good-looking. Thinks he's cool. What a nerd.

Or take that little kid walking on top of the railing out there. The train has stopped on the bridge, so I could jump off and save him if I wanted. But why should I? I might fall in myself. It's a long way down to the river. The water is deep. I could drown, or skin my knees getting out of the train.

Nah. It's his problem. He is showing off. He should know better. He's going to fall in and it will serve him right.

Or take this guy sitting next to the nerd. A real weirdo with purple hair, a nose ring and . . . wait for it. Yes, really. A parrot sitting on his shoulder. He must think he's a pirate or something.

The stupid parrot can talk. Not much. Just a bit. One sentence is all it can say. The weirdo says crazy things back to the parrot. I can hardly believe it.

'Say it again, Sam,' screeches the parrot.

'I hate apple pies,' says the weirdo.

'Say it again, Sam,' screeches the parrot.

'This place stinks,' says the weirdo.

I look out of the window at the pathetic kid tottering along on the edge of the railway fence. Still showing off.

I lean out of the door. 'Stupid idiot,' I yell.

The little kid looks up with panic on his face. My voice has startled him. Suddenly he is scared. His knees start to wobble. He holds out his arms like a tightrope-walker but it only makes things worse. He flaps his arms like a crazy bird.

Oh no. Slowly, slowly, slowly, he starts to topple backwards.

Everyone in the train is looking now.

'Aaagggh.' Over he goes. Twisting and turning in the air. Down, down, down. *Kersplash*. He disappears beneath the surface of the muddy Yarra River.

We all jump out of the train and stare over the

edge. Nothing. Nothing but bubbles. He has gone. For ever. No he hasn't. There he is. He's thrashing around. No, he's gone again. He can't swim. He's going to drown.

Everyone stands there frozen. Except the weirdo with the parrot. He runs over to a box on the railing. He opens it. He pulls out a lifebuoy. He throws it in.

What a shot. The lifebuoy lands right next to the drowning kid, who looks like he is going down for the last time. He grabs onto it and starts kicking. He kicks and kicks until he reaches the bank of the river.

The train driver and a few others scramble down to pull him out.

The crowd from the train goes wild. They cheer and yell. They pat the weirdo on the back. Then they lift him over their heads. He has this great big grin on his face. Anyone would think he had saved the world or something. The parrot flutters around over his head.

The train driver starts to carry the little kid up from the river. We all have to wait for them to get back.

When they arrive we gather around for a look. There is quite a racket. 'Quiet, everyone,' says the train driver. 'This guy here,' he says, pointing to the weirdo, 'should get a medal. His quick thinking saved the day. He grabbed the lifebuoy and threw it in.'

'Big deal,' I say.

Everyone falls quiet. They turn and look at me. Especially the train driver. He is really angry. He looks at me as if I am a load of dog poop. 'Some people,' he says, 'stood by and did nothing.'

An old lady pushes through to the front and puts her face close to mine. 'He caused it all,' she said. 'He yelled out and made the poor boy fall in the first place.'

'If you can't say something useful,' says the train driver, 'better to say nothing at all.'

The crowd all started to mumble and grumble and abuse me.

'Scum.'

'No-hoper.'

'Layabout.'

'Good for nothing.'

This makes my blood boil. 'I didn't do anything,' I spit out.

'Precisely,' says the stupid train driver. 'But this bloke did.' They all start patting the weirdo on the back again.

It is sickening. All that fuss over nothing.

Suddenly the parrot flies off into some trees and disappears. The weirdo watches it go with a smile. He doesn't seem to care that he has lost his stupid parrot.

And I don't care either. Good riddance to it.

2

In the end we all have to walk to the next station because they can't start the train. I hurry along in front so that I don't have to listen to everyone telling the weirdo how good he is.

Far off in the trees I hear the parrot screech. It is an awful noise. No one seems to notice it except me. It gives me the creeps. I have a nasty feeling I haven't seen the last of that parrot.

I get to the station before anyone else. The other passengers are all waiting for the old lady and helping to carry the little kid who fell in the river.

I am mad. I am angry. I decide to do a bit of damage. I go into the dunny and look for something to smash up.

I try to rip a dunny seat off but it won't come. I pull and pull but it is bolted on tight. My hands

are hurting something awful. I let all my feelings out.
I curse and I yell. I swear something terrible.

Then I give the dunny seat a kick but it won't
budge. Suddenly I see something grouse. It is a
dunny seat for little squirts. It is small and titchy, if
you know what I mean. If you were a gnome or
something it would be just the shot.

This ought to be easy. I grab the wooden seat and
give it a yank. *Snap.* It is only held on with plastic
bolts and they break just like that. No worries.

I hold the little dunny seat up in the air and am
just about to smash it down on the ground when I
see something. A pair of shoes. With feet in them.
Someone is in the next cubicle.

It could be the law. I stand there with the dunny
seat held up over my head. I am as still as a statue.
Then I decide to run for it. But suddenly, *whomp.*
I slip on some water and down I go.

And down comes the dunny seat. Straight over
my head. Yow. Ouch, ooh. Geez, it hurts. And it
won't come off. I pull and yank and everything but
it won't move.

I jump up onto my feet and take a gawk in the
mirror. I stare and stare. No, no no. My head is
jammed inside the toilet seat. My eyes and ears and

nose poke out of the hole. And the lid is flapping up above me. *Whump*. The lid falls down and hits me fair on the back of my head. Ow. This is my unlucky day. My skull is killing me.

The shoes in the next cubicle are moving. It is time for me to leave. Just then, without warning, the door swings open. It is the train driver. How did he get here so quick?

'You're fast for an old guy,' I say.

'And you have a fast tongue,' he says. 'I've been listening to you cursing and swearing. And you made that little boy fall off the bridge.'

'Get lost, Pops,' I say.

'You should think before you speak,' he says. 'You have a mean tongue.'

The dunny seat is hurting my face. I have no time for his lectures. 'Get a life, Grandad,' I say.

The train driver goes red in the face. For a moment I think his head is about to explode but it doesn't. He stomps off out of the dunny. I sure fixed *him* up. If there's one thing I know how to do it's to make people feel small. I'm real good at it.

Then I notice something.

The parrot. It is sitting on the cubicle looking down at me.

Screech.

A little shiver runs down my spine. I don't like this parrot. I look around for something to throw at it but there is nothing about.

'Beat it, Feather Head,' I yell.

The parrot flies up into the air flapping its wings like crazy. And I run out of the dunny as quick as I can go. The toilet seat is starting to hurt my face. I have to hang on to the lid to stop it banging me on the nut every time I take a step.

I burst out onto the platform. The sun hurts my eyes but I squint and see that the train has arrived. And it is ready to go. Quick as a flash I jump onto the train. The toilet lid bangs down and hits me like a hammer. 'Ouch, ooh, ow.'

Things are bad. But they get worse. Everyone is looking at me. Sitting there on the train with a toilet seat jammed on my head. There is no sign of the weirdo. His parrot is gone. But the nerd is trying to smother a laugh. This is the worst day of my life.

The train is about to leave. The doors start to close. But before they do, a last-minute passenger steps onto the train. *Flies* onto the train I should say. It is the parrot. It seems to be staring at me. I don't like the look of it.

The parrot gives a bit of a jump and sits up on the seat next to me.

3

This is unbelievable. This is unreal. What is going on here? First I get a dunny seat stuck around my face and now this little parrot is following me around. I don't get it. And neither does anyone else. Every eye is looking at my face or this little parrot.

'What are you lot gawking at?' I say. 'Why don't you mind your own business?'

The parrot gives a squawk.

Okay. I know what to do with this parrot. I will chuck it out of the window. I make a dive for the parrot but it is too quick and it dodges away. I fall over and graze my knee. I make another lunge but again it is too quick for me and it flaps up onto the luggage rack. I slip onto the lap of an old lady.

'Careful,' she says crossly.

'Get lost, Grandma,' I say.

Squawk, goes the parrot, and everyone laughs.

Right. I'm going to fix them. They have embarrassed me. I will embarrass them back.

There is a blonde aged about sixteen sitting as far

away from me as she can get. She is looking at my toilet seat out of the corner of her eye. I put my face up close to hers. I look straight at her. 'Give us a kiss, darling,' I say.

Squawk, says the parrot.

The girl does not like this suggestion. Her nose starts to twitch.

I put my face next to hers and make little kissing noises. 'You are a little sweetheart, aren't you?' I say.

Squawk, says the parrot.

'Leave her alone,' says the nerd.

'Yes,' says someone else. They all start to mumble and grumble at me.

'You are all wimps,' I say. 'I reckon I might have to teach you all a lesson.'

Squawk, shrieks the parrot. It is almost as if it doesn't approve of what I am doing. Like a nagging parent ticking me off.

I let go of the toilet lid and shake a finger at the parrot. *Whump*, my toilet lid falls down and dongs me on the head again.

Everyone in the carriage laughs. Everyone. Even the parrot seems to think it's funny. Okay. This is war. I will tell them what I think of them.

'You are all snobs,' I say. 'Stuck-up, snotty snobs.'

Squawk, says the parrot.

They all pretend not to hear me. They look at their papers or stare out of the window. A tall skinny guy is nibbling a sandwich. The filling looks like horse droppings. 'Hey, stupid,' I say. 'Can I have a bit of that horse manure?'

He tries to ignore me, so I bend over and take a bit of sandwich. I chew it quickly. Actually it's not too bad. 'That was lovely,' I say. 'Can I have some more?'

A woman with a baby in a pram does not like this. 'Leave him alone, you horrible boy,' she says.

'You're an ugly cow,' I say to her. 'Why don't you mind your own business?' That fixes her up. She goes as red as a beetroot.

Every time I say something the parrot squawks. It is starting to get on my nerves.

A very old codger is sitting in the corner with earplugs stuffed in his ears. He is trying not to look at me. I can hear the tune because he has it up so loud. I know this song. My old grandma sings it all the time when she is doing the dishes.

I start to sing and dance around in front of him, pulling funny faces. I know this rotten song backwards. I pull a leering face while I sing.

Her eyes they shone like the diamonds,
You'd think she was Queen of the land,
And her hair hung over her shoulder,
Tied up with a black velvet band.

I sing all of the verses, making the old boy as embarrassed as anything. All the time the parrot goes *squawk, squawk, squawk*. Finally I stop because the train pulls into the station. We have arrived. Flinders Street. The middle of the city. I wait until everyone has stepped off. The parrot waits too. It is just sitting there next to me with its little wings flapping every now and then. I have to lose it. And quick.

I wait until everyone is off the train. I wait until it is just about to pull out of the station. I hold down my toilet lid and leap off. But I am not quick enough. The parrot almost seems to read my mind. It hits the platform at the same time as me. There is no way it is going to let me shake it off.

The parrot follows me along the platform. I feel like a pirate out of some old movie. Ridiculous. That's how I feel. The stupid bird flaps up in the air and tries to land on my shoulder but I brush it off.

Talk about embarrassing. Travellers stop to look.

A boy with a toilet seat stuck on his head, running away from a parrot. What a sight. Everyone starts to laugh. They think it is some sort of a show. Rats, rats, rats. I am a joke. I am pathetic. I have to get this stupid thing off my head. And I have to get rid of the parrot.

I kick out at the parrot with my foot. I kick hard enough to send it into orbit. But it is too fast. It flaps out of the way and my leg goes flying up over my head. I lose my balance and *bang*, down I go onto the platform. And *bang* goes the toilet lid onto my head.

Oh, agony, agony. I have to get this thing off my head. I will have to get to a hospital. It's the only way. Someone will have to cut the toilet seat away from my face.

The crowd stare down at me, laughing. I need help. I need someone to drive me to a hospital. A little old woman comes over to me and bends down. She smiles at me and helps me up. 'You poor boy,' she says. 'Can I help you?'

I go to say yes. But 'yes' does not come out.

Say it again, Sam, screeches the parrot.

'Get lost, Grandma,' I say.

The old woman lets go of my arm and *plonk*, I fall back down again.

145

'You have a bad mouth,' she says. She wags a finger at me and starts to hurry off through the crowd.

Oh no. This is no good. This is terrible. Why did I tell her to get lost? I will never get to hospital this way. People are staring down at me. Surely someone will have mercy on me. I look up at the staring faces. I will ask them for help.

Suddenly the parrot speaks. *Say it again, Sam.*

'What are you lot gawking at?' I say to the passers-by. 'Why don't you all mind your own business.'

The onlookers mumble and grumble. They say things like, 'What a rude kid' and 'The nerve of it'.

They are all going off and leaving me. No, no no. Don't go. I didn't mean to say that. I will call out to them and ask for help. 'You are all snobs,' I say. 'Stuck up, snotty snobs.'

The crowd hurry off. Soon the platform is empty.

Why did I say all those things? I didn't mean to be rude. Why am I insulting people? My mouth seems to work on its own. It won't say what I want it to. I look down at the parrot. It just sits there. Watching. Saying nothing. This has something to do with the parrot talking.

I pick myself up and head out of the station.

I must get to hospital. I could catch a taxi but I only have two dollars. That won't get me far. I show my ticket and go out onto the street. There is a horse hitched up to a stagecoach. It's there to take tourists and little kids for rides around the town. Maybe the guy who drives it will help. He has a kind face. He is busy shovelling up horse manure and putting it into a bin.

He looks up when I approach. He stares at my toilet seat and smiles.

Say it again, Sam, screeches the parrot.

I open my mouth to speak. 'Hey, stupid,' I say. 'Can I have a bit of that horse manure?'

The smile falls from his face. He does not like being called stupid. 'Sure, toilet head,' he says. He looks down at his shovel and the pile of sloppy steaming manure. Then he throws it straight in my face.

Oh, yuck. The stinking stuff is in my eyes and ears and nose. I start clawing it away with my fingers. It is so foul that I think I'm going to faint.

The guy is picking up another shovelful. I must tell him to stop.

Say it again, Sam, screeches the parrot.

'That was lovely,' I say. 'Can I have some more?'

147

What? What? Why did I say that? Oh, no. *Sploosh*. He lets me have it again.

I stagger away as quickly as I can, before he has time to scoop up another shovelful.

The parrot follows after me.

4

People in the street make way for me. They avoid me like the plague. I don't blame them. A guy with a toilet seat on his head. Covered in stinking horse manure and followed by a stupid parrot that flaps around just over his head. They probably think I am a lunatic or something.

My mind is spinning. Why am I saying these things? Each time I have spoken, the parrot has said *Say it again, Sam*. What's going on? My own words start to buzz around in my head. I said, *Hey, stupid, can I have a bit of that horse manure?* I have heard that before.

Then it hits me. It's what I said on the train. To the tall skinny bloke with the sandwich. And, *Get lost, Grandma*. I said that on the train too. And, *What are you lot gawking at? Why don't you all mind your own business*. I also said that on the train.

The parrot is making me repeat myself. It has remembered every word I said. Like a tape recorder. And now it's making me say them all again. When I don't want to. Parrots can copy what people say. But this one is making me copy myself.

What else did I say? I can't remember. But one thing's certain. I have to get away from this parrot. And quick.

I look around. There must be someone who can take me to hospital. Someone who can save me. A policewoman. She is giving parking tickets to some bikies. They are great big blokes with beer bellies and beards. They do not like getting parking tickets.

I wouldn't normally talk to the police. But this is an emergency. The police are there to help. That is what they always say. I will give it a go and ask her to take me to the hospital. I will be very polite to her. Very polite indeed.

She looks up as I approach. She starts to grin when she sees my toilet seat. 'Yes?' she says.

I open my mouth to speak. But the parrot gets in first.

Say it again, Sam.

'You're an ugly cow,' I say to the policewoman. 'Why don't you mind your own business?'

149

Oh, no, no, no. The parrot has made me repeat my words. The policewoman steps towards me. 'You are under arrest,' she says.

'What for, ugly?' says the bikie with the biggest beer gut. 'Why don't you leave him alone? He doesn't need a licence to walk around with a toilet seat on his head. And there is no law against telling the truth, either.'

The gang members kick their bikes into action. Before I can blink Beer Gut has lifted me up and plonked me on the back of his bike. In a flash we are speeding down the street with the rest of the gang thundering after us. The policewoman is yelling at us. But we don't hear what she says because the motorbikes are roaring.

This is good. This is better. I am with *my* sort of people now. They are rough. They are tough. They speak their minds. They do not mind people who say what they think.

We weave in and out of the streets. People stare at me and Beer Gut. A big fat bikie and a guy with a toilet seat on his head.

Some of the bikies have their women on the back. The sheilas wrap their arms around their blokes' waists and hang on like crazy. One bikie has a little parrot sitting on the back seat. Oh, no, the parrot again. It is still with me. It will never let me go.

The bikies screech to a stop in a back alley filled with rubbish bins.

The parrot hops down from its little perch on the seat and stretches its wings. All of the bikies stare at the parrot. 'I like your mate,' says Beer Gut. 'Can it fight?' He tries to grab the parrot but it's too quick for him.

Beer Gut gives up on the parrot and looks at me. 'You helped us,' he says. 'How can we help you?'

At last someone is going to help me. I smile at Beer Gut just as the parrot starts to talk.

Say it again, Sam.

'Give us a kiss, darling,' I say to Beer Gut.

Beer Gut does not like this suggestion. His beard starts to bristle. 'What?' he yells.

I put my face next to his and make little kissing noises. 'You are a little sweetheart, aren't you?' I say.

I try to stop my mouth talking but I can't. I hold my mouth with my fingers but it is no good. My tongue just keeps flapping away saying one mean thing after another. Beer Gut is getting madder and madder. The gang close in around me. 'You are all wimps,' I say. 'I reckon I might have to teach you all a lesson.'

'Wimps, are we?' says Beer Gut. He lifts up my toilet seat and slams it down on my head. That is all I remember because I am knocked out by the blow. It's goodnight for me for quite a while.

5

When I wake up I am upside down. Things do not look too good. In fact things do not look anything at all because everything is black. And smelly. I am upside down and I stink of dead fish and rotting cabbages. I am in a rubbish bin. I can hardly breathe because of the terrible stench.

Somehow or other I wriggle out of the bin and crash down onto the ground. The toilet seat is still on my face but the lid bit has broken off. At least I won't have that banging me on the nut any more.

The parrot, however, is sitting on a window-ledge watching me. Saying nothing. I want to yell at it. But I can't say anything because it will start talking and I might start saying something that I wish I hadn't.

I am covered in stinking rubbish and something

yellow is dribbling down my face. I try to pull off the toilet seat but it hurts too much. I push and struggle but it is going to rip my ear off. There's only one thing left to do. I will go home. Grandma is a crabby old girl but she will help me. She's used to me saying mean things and probably won't even notice if the parrot makes me insult her.

I fish around in my pocket for my train ticket.

It is gone. So are my two dollars. Beer Gut has taken them both.

Oh, rats. Rats, rats, rats. What else can go wrong? Now I can't get home. I will have to try and talk the ticket collector into letting me on without a ticket. But then the parrot will screech, *Say it again, Sam*. And I will say something rude and they will chase me off.

I trudge back towards Flinders Street Station. People stare at me. People avoid me. They see a smelly boy with a toilet seat on his face and a parrot flapping along above his head.

Finally the parrot and I arrive at the station. I am tired. I am scared. I am sick of saying rude things to people. How am I going to get onto the train without a ticket? I look around at the crowd. People are staring at me. Suddenly something snaps in my mind. I will tell them all what I think of them. I will yell. I will swear. I don't care about anything any more.

I stand on the top step and open my mouth.

Say it again, Sam, screeches the parrot.

Oh no. What now?

I start to sing. That's what. A happy little song that Grandma sings. Please, parrot, please don't make me sing. I try to keep my mouth shut but it is no good. I sing at the top of my voice.

> *Her eyes they shone like the diamonds,*
> *You'd think she was Queen of the land,*
> *And her hair hung over her shoulder,*
> *Tied up with a black velvet band.*

The crowd stop and look. But they are not mad at me. And they do not think I am mad. They are smiling. They think it's a show. They think I'm a busker. They clap and laugh at me and the toilet seat and the parrot, which is doing a little dance on top of my head.

I keep singing. I sing the next verse. And the next one. Finally I finish the song. I give a little bow. I'm quite proud of myself actually.

People throw money on the ground. They liked the show. Twenty cents. One dollar. Two dollars. Not bad. Not bad at all. I scoop up all the coins and when the crowd has gone I count them. Fifteen dollars and forty-five cents. Just the ticket. Just enough *for* a ticket actually.

I go over to the ticket machine and buy a one-way ticket to Colac.

I jump onto the train and sit down just as it moves off. The parrot sits on my shoulder. The passengers stare at me but not in a mean way. I see some of the people who threw money to me. The ones who liked the show. I also see the nerd. He's there too.

Well, I'm not going to say anything. The parrot will only make me insult them. I stare out of the window and think about my troubles. If only I could get rid of this toilet seat without ripping my ears off. If only the parrot would give me a break and go away.

The train rumbles on for quite a while. Finally it stops on a bridge. It's the same bridge where the little kid was walking on top of the railing.

There he is again. I can't believe it. The same kid is walking on the railings in exactly the same spot. Oh, what? It can't be true. My mind freezes. I can't think what to do. I can't take it in.

The nerd isn't frozen though. Not him. He rushes over to the door and opens it. 'Be careful,' he yells at the top of his voice.

The little kid looks up with panic on his face. The nerd's voice has startled him. Suddenly he is scared. His knees start to wobble. He holds out his arms like a tightrope-walker but it only makes things worse. He flaps his arms like a crazy bird.

Oh, no. Slowly, slowly, slowly, he starts to topple backwards.

Everyone in the train is looking now.

'Aaagggh.' Over he goes. Twisting and turning in the air. Down, down, down. *Kersplash.* He disappears beneath the surface of the muddy Yarra River.

We all jump out of the train and stare over the edge. Nothing. Nothing but bubbles. He has gone. For ever. No he hasn't. There he is. He's thrashing around. No, he's gone again. He can't swim. He's going to drown.

Everyone stands there frozen. Except the nerd. The hero. He runs over to a box on the railing. He opens it. But there's nothing there. They have not replaced the lifebuoy. There's nothing to throw. We

all look around for something that will float. Anything. But there is not so much as a matchstick on
that bridge.

The nerd starts trying to pull at a railing from the
bridge but it won't come off. The little kid sinks out
of sight again. It's a long way down. Everyone is too
scared to jump in and save him. And there's nothing
to throw.

Except.

My toilet seat.

I push and push like mad. But I can't shift it. The
toilet seat won't budge. And the pain is terrible. My
ears are starting to bleed. Oh, oh, oh, it hurts, it
hurts. But I can't stop. The kid is drowning. I have
to get this toilet seat off my head. *Sploosh.* The toilet
seat comes off. So does a piece of my ear. There is
blood everywhere. The pain is terrible.

'He's going down again,' yells the nerd. 'He's going
to drown. Someone do something.'

I rush to the railing and throw over the toilet seat.
What a shot. The toilet seat lands right next to the
drowning kid, who looks like he's going down for
the last time. The kid grabs onto the toilet seat. It's
just like a lifebuoy. He starts kicking. He kicks and
kicks until he reaches the bank of the river.

The train driver and a few others scramble down to pull him out.

The crowd goes crazy. A nurse from the next carriage has picked up the piece of my ear and put it in a bottle. 'They can sew it back on,' she says. She ties a bandage around my head and although it hurts I can tell you that it feels a lot better than a toilet seat.

Everyone pats me on the back. They cheer and shout. They say they have never seen such courage. 'You are a real hero,' says an old lady. 'They should give you a medal.' She looks at all the others. 'He almost tore off his own ear to save that little boy.'

'It was nothing,' I say. 'Anyone would have done the same thing.'

Everyone smiles at me. I smile to myself. They like what I said. So do I.

I look around. The parrot has gone. No, there it is. It is flying over the river towards the road on the other side. It is heading for a bikie who has been pulled over by the police. He is a big guy with a beer gut. He is shaking a fist at the police. I wonder what he is saying.

I hope it is something nice. Because I bet that stupid ... er, lovely little parrot is squawking its head off every time he speaks.

About the Author

Paul Jennings is Australia's multi-award-winning master of madness. The Paul Jennings phenomenon began with publication of *Unreal!* in 1985. Since then, his stories have been devoured all around the world.

In 2007, Paul's book sales surpassed eight million copies. In 1995 he was made a member of the Order of Australia for Services to Literature and in 2001 was awarded the Dromkeen Medal for his significant contribution to the appreciation and development of children's literature. He lives in Warrnambool, Victoria, on twenty-one hectares of coastal land which he is turning into a wildlife refuge by replacing the introduced plants with species that once made up the original native forest.

COME EXPLORING AT

www.penguin.com.au

AND

www.puffin.com.au

FOR

Author and illustrator profiles

Book extracts

Reviews

Competitions

Activities, games and puzzles

Advice for budding authors

Tips for parents

Teacher resources